Also by Trae Dorn

The Mia Graves Series
The Witch and the Rose
Bloody Damn Rite
Shadowcasting
Buried Memories
The Perfect Host

Peregrine Lake Series
(with art by Ethan Flanagan)
Welcome to Peregrine Lake

Other Comics and Graphic Novels
UnCONventional
The Chronicles of Crosarth

Mia Graves Book Two

BLOODY DAMN RITE

TRAE DORN

NERD &TIE

www.nerdandtie.com
www.traedorn.com

For Crysta.
Because of course it is.

Prologue

A cold autumn wind whipped through Parrish Mills as Emma stepped out onto the street. She ran her hand through her short, dyed hair and sighed. The bass was thumping from the music in the bar behind her so loudly she could still feel it in her chest, and it was just too much. It had been a terrible night out; She was tired, her back hurt, and Megan had run off with some guy who still thought crypto was a thing.

"I really need to find better friends," she said quietly to the empty street.

Emma pulled out her phone and glanced at the time. It was well after midnight, and she couldn't really afford a rideshare home. It would probably only be a twenty minute walk back to her dorm on the Garrity University campus. That was really her only move at this point.

Emma shivered and quietly cursed herself for not bringing a coat. The desolate street was dimly lit by flickering streetlights, casting eerie shadows that danced along the pavement. A sense of unease settled deep within her, but she shook it off, reminding herself that she was just being paranoid.

As she walked briskly, the rhythmic sound of her footsteps echoed around her. A flash of movement drew her eye, and for a moment she swore she saw the silhouette of a man in the shadows. When she turned to look, it was gone as if it had never been there.

"Get a grip, Emma," she mumbled to herself. "Just your eyes playing tricks on you."

She couldn't help but feel like she was being followed, like something was hunting her. Emma quickened her pace, her heart pounding in her chest. She desperately tried to convince herself that it was all in her head, that there was nothing to be afraid of. But the nagging feeling of being watched only intensified with each step she took.

As she turned a corner onto yet another dimly lit street, Emma's senses heightened. The smell of dampness filled the air, and a chill ran down her spine. She could feel the presence closing in, lurking just beyond her line of sight. Panic set in, causing her to break out into a cold sweat.

"Who's there?" she called out, her voice quivering.

Silence.

Emma's heart raced as she continued to walk, now even faster. She pulled out her phone, and started to key in 9 and 1 as she began to move faster. She had to make a decision soon – take the long way around that was better lit, or the direct path through the park. It was hard to tell which was more dangerous.

"Oh my dear, why are you in such a hurry?" a deep voice echoed in the night, seemingly coming from nowhere. Emma stopped in her tracks, fear creeping like ice through her veins.

"Who is that?" she yelled into the night.

"Just someone who admires what he sees," the voice replied with a sinister chuckle. "I've been watching you tonight, Emma."

"You... you don't scare me," Emma lied, moving forward again.

"Oh, you don't need to be scared my dear," the voice laughed. "I'm not here to hurt you, I'm here to offer you a gift."

"Don't want it, you can keep it," Emma said, moving faster.

"Oh my dear, you don't really have a choice," the voice answered.

Emma suddenly felt an arm grab her from behind, and she was pushed against the wall, unable to see her attacker. She tried to struggle, but found she couldn't move.

"Now my dear, this part might hurt a bit," the voice said quietly, now just a whisper in her ear. Emma felt a sharp pain in the side of her neck, and the world went black.

Chapter 1

Mia wrapped her arms around herself, pulling the jacket tightly around her shoulders. It was a minor bulwark against the cold night, but it's what she had. Another gust of wind buffeted her, sending her dark curls in front of her eyes, obscuring her vision.

"I still think it's a weird idea," Sarah said, as she strode alongside, a smile on the edge of her lips. "I'm genuinely shocked you went through with it."

Sarah was roughly the same height as Mia, but walked with a confidence that made her seem taller. Strong, beautiful, and dressed in a warm leather jacket, her long, chestnut brown hair seemed to flow behind her in the wind like a banner announcing her presence. Sarah was everything Mia loved in this world, the one shining light she'd found. They'd met as teenagers, both fighting to survive on their own. Most people thought Sarah was cold and harsh, but Mia knew the truth. Mia knew that Sarah was the softest, warmest person who walked the Earth, and the rest was just an act to keep the world at bay.

Sarah would give anything to keep Mia safe. *Why does it feel like she already has?*

"It's not weird, it's brilliant," Mia laughed. "Building sigils and runes into tattoos means you *always* have the spells you need at hand. All you have to do is periodically charge them up, and you're golden. No additional components needed. You can do specific spells, like protection – or, like, keeping yourself warm in the cold. Or you can just make them do things like help you channel magic better, like this one does!"

Mia rolled up her left sleeve, revealing an intricate tattoo on her forearm.

"Yeah, but then anyone can see what you're doing!" Sarah replied. "Like you're advertising what you've got on hand."

"I could still do *other* spells, Sarah." Mia rolled her eyes, and playfully poked at Sarah's side. "And, like, if someone knows every obscure version of every spell by seeing the symbols on me, dude would *also* recognize it if I started doing it the long way too."

"Sounds like a shortcut and an unnecessary risk. What happens if you accidentally activate one in your sleep," Sarah said, shaking her head.

"Building a safeguard against that is pretty easy, and besides," Mia paused, grabbing Sarah's hand and pulling her close. "You'll just have to find ways to tire me out so much that I can't."

Sarah gently brushed Mia's long, dark hair out of her face and smiled. "I love you Mia Graves."

"I love you too, Sarah Masters," Mia smiled, pulling Sarah into a kiss while they stood on the broken Boston sidewalk. *I'm in Boston? I feel like I've left this place already. I shouldn't be here. Why do I feel like that? Didn't this happen already?*

"Come on Ms. Spell-hacker, we need to get moving if we're going to get down to the warehouse before midnight," Sarah said with a wink. "Tonight is going to be amazing. Unlike your weird tattoo thing, this is *actually* a brilliant idea."

Wait, what's tonight? What night is this? Something was wrong. *Why is this all so cloudy? Why do I feel like I've done this before.*

The world seemed to flicker a little, and Sarah almost seemed to shift. Her face grew harder, and her hair shifted and was suddenly shorter. Sarah's jacket suddenly looked more dirty and worn.

"What is happening," Mia gasped, finally saying something that didn't feel like an old memory. "Oh god, this is that night. This is *that night.*"

Sarah seemed to sigh, and sat down on the sidewalk. "That's not something you said, I hate it when a dream does that…"

I'm dreaming. This is a dream. This is all just a memory.

Mia blinked the building tears from her eyes. "Maybe I should have said lots of things I didn't that night. Maybe I should have told you I was having doubts. Why was I so stupid."

"We were both stupid," Sarah said, looking at the ground. "We were idiots looking to get high in literally the most dangerous way possible. I feel like if we'd started using *heroin* it would have been smarter than what we did."

"I kept pushing you to escalate," Mia replied, sitting down on the curb next to Sarah. Mia suddenly didn't feel cold anymore. Glancing at her arms, she saw that they were now covered in tattoos instead of just the single one that had been there a minute before. "Giving over to more powerful entities every time. Robby had already *died* when we got to this point."

"But we kept going," Sarah said, shaking her head. "It was just easier to escape into more of this bullshit than deal with what happened."

"Do you want to know the worst part?" Mia said quietly. "I still miss it sometimes. I couldn't risk letting myself slip back into it, and it's one of the reasons I left Boston. I knew if I relapsed, I might end up hurting you even more."

"God, I wish the real Mia was brave enough to tell me that," Sarah exhaled. "It's almost heartbreaking to hear it come out of some idealized version of you from my subconscious instead."

"Uh… I *am* the real Mia," Mia said, her eyebrows furrowed in confusion. "I'm the one that's having this dream."

****

Mia awoke with a start, her chest heaving as she struggled to catch her breath.

She blinked, squinting through the slivers of sunlight that pierced the tattered curtain hanging over her small studio apartment's single window. The taste of stale sweat and lingering desire clung to her tongue, filling her mouth with an acrid tang. Reality came slamming back into her full force. It had been almost two years since she saw last saw Sarah, and over a year since she'd left Boston.

God, yesterday was the second anniversary of that night in the warehouse, Mia realized. *How did I almost forget?*

Lying beside her, tangled in the musty sheets, was Bobbi. The twenty-one year old's flushed cheeks and tousled hair evidence of the previous night's feverish revelry. Mia let out a quiet exhale, her memory of the night before clouded by a lustful haze. It was always nice to wake up next to Bobbi. Nothing was complicated with her. Bobbi lived in the ordinary world and lived an ordinary life, unaware of the darkness that always crept along the edge.

And it was nice to just escape to that every once and a while.

Sure, it probably wasn't actually all that *healthy* for Mia, but she'd done far worse things to her own body during her twenty-eight years of life. This seemed like a minor transgression in proportion.

That and it always felt nice to be wanted.

"Shit," Mia muttered under her breath as she glanced at the battered alarm clock on her bedside table. The clock glared back at her like a crimson accusation, mocking her for forgetting to turn her alarm on the night before. She was going to be late for work if she didn't get moving immediately, and Zelda Markov would not be happy if her store didn't open on time. With a sudden urgency, Mia threw off the thin blanket and scrambled to her feet, ignoring the dull ache that lingered in her limbs.

"Bobbi, wake up." Mia's voice wavered between annoyance and desperation as she shook the younger woman's shoulder. "You gotta go. Now."

Bobbi groaned, rubbing her eyes as she blinked up at Mia. "What's the rush? We've got all day to stay in bed, don't we?"

"*You've* got all day. I don't. I'm an adult with a job. It's a Tuesday. Get dressed and get moving." Mia didn't bother hiding her irritation as she grabbed a skirt from one of the piles of clothes on the floor, hoping it was clean enough.

"Fine, fine." Bobbi sighed, stretching lazily across the bed before sitting up. She began to hunt for her scattered clothes while tying back her shoulder length red hair. Mia could tell Bobbi was staring at her tattoos again. Bobbi always told Mia how cool they were, but had no idea the intricate markings that danced across her limbs, chest and back were a series of embedded spells. "You never tell me what these mean," she mused, tracing a finger along one of the symbols.

"And you've never told me your middle name. We both like the mystery." Mia's voice was curt as she pulled on her black tank top, trying to avoid explaining a world full of monsters and darkness. Bobbi was a college kid who didn't need to know about the real things that went bump in the night. Hell, some days Mia wished *she* didn't.

"Alright, alright." Bobbi rolled her eyes, pulling on her own clothes with exaggerated slowness. "I'm going, I'm going." Bobbi stopped for a moment while shrugging on a flannel shirt, "I know this might sound odd, but I'm going up to my family's land next month for deer camp. It might be fun if you came along?"

"You want me to come with you... deer hunting?" Mia asked, raising an eyebrow. "What exactly would I do?"

"Have sex with me in a cabin at night when I'm done deer hunting with my cousins?" Bobbi answered, winking.

"Yeah, no... I think I'll sit that one out," Mia said, rolling her eyes. "Now I need to get going so..."

"Fine fine, I won't show you photos of my new rifle," Bobbi said, raising her hands. "I'll go – don't worry."

"Thank you," Mia said, her tone clipped as she grabbed her messenger bag. Mia paused, taking a breath. "Sorry Bobbi, I'm just stressed out. Last night was nice."

Bobbi smiled, brushing a lock of Mia's long, dark curly hair out of her eyes. "Yeah, it was. I'll text you."

Bobbi kissed Mia on the cheek, and stepped out the door into the blinding morning sun with a bounce. She was down the block in almost an instant.

Mia was almost jealous of that kind of energy.

She knew she should probably stop sleeping with Bobbi, but Mia had a hard time saying no when she showed up at her door at two in the morning. They were different people at very different points in their lives, and none of this was healthy. But sometimes an unhealthy distraction helped her forget, if only for a moment, a past that still haunted her dreams.

Mia stepped out her door into the parking lot of her apartment building, letting the cold morning air surround her. The building was run down, with each unit directly exiting outside. The walkway to the second floor creaked overhead as one of her neighbors seemed to be taking a walk of shame home.

Mia sometimes wondered what her life would be like if she'd gone to college. Or graduated high school. Or not been homeless and on her own at fifteen.

Her breath hung visibly in the air, as a hazy mist clung to the world. Mrs. Hendricks gave a small wave from her front porch across the way, and Mia returned it before practically darting down the street. The neighborhood was a mishmash of poorly built student housing for the local university and historic homes. Parrish Mills was your average college town nestled along the Wabash River in Northern Indiana, a small outpost of green surrounded by corn. It had been Mia's home for a little over a year, and she'd found comfort in the simple mundanity of the place.

The aroma of freshly brewed coffee wafted from a small café as Mia neared, its warm glow beckoning her inside. She pushed open the door, the bell above jangling merrily, and scanned the interior for a familiar face. Riley Whittaker sat at their usual corner table, her long blonde hair contrasting sharply against the dark leather of the booth. A steaming cup of black coffee sat before her, and she looked up, grinning as Mia approached.

"Running late again, I see," Riley teased, gesturing for Mia to sit down.

"No sitting, must keep moving. Wasn't exactly a peaceful night," Mia replied, her voice tinged with annoyance as she bounced nervously, trying to keep the blood flow moving. "Bobbi came over unexpectedly."

"Ah, Bobbi. That's what, the eighth time this month? You could always say no to her." Riley raised an eyebrow as she took a sip of her coffee. Her blue eyes sparkled with mischief, but Mia could also sense the underlying concern.

"Could I? Yes. Should I? Definitely. Will I? Who the fuck knows," Mia muttered, rubbing at one of her tattoos absently. She ordered a latte at the counter, her eye constantly on the clock, and tried to shake off any residual regret.

"Hey," Riley said with a smirk, reaching over to grip Mia's hand. "Could be worse, at least Bobbi's a living person. You could be hooking up with a ghost… again."

"God that was over a year ago," Mia responded, with a laugh. "You sleep with one ghost and no one lets you live it down."

"If by 'no one,' you mean me, then yes," Riley continued, taking another sip, "but if you feel like going for round two, there are at least a couple dozen other ghosts in my house you could take a run at."

Mia snorted, allowing herself a genuine laugh at the idea. Riley lived in the notoriously haunted Rose House, and while the young professor had made peace with the spirits that inhabited the place, they still creeped Mia out a bit. "I'll keep that in mind."

"Good," Riley said firmly, taking another swig of her coffee. "Now, let's get you to work before your boss sends out a search party."

"Agreed," Mia replied, as her order arrived at the counter. Grabbing her coffee, Mia walked swiftly out the door, with Riley close behind.

The morning sun cast a warm golden glow on the aged brick buildings that lined downtown. Mia and Riley walked side by side, their strides in sync as they traversed the familiar path toward Zelda Markov's bookstore. A cool autumn breeze rustled the turning leaves overhead, bringing a chill to the crisp morning.

"Can't believe I'm running late to work again," Mia muttered, her fingers fiddling with the strap of her messenger bag nervously.

"Hey, don't worry about it," Riley reassured her. "I'll let you in on a little secret – I've been late to more than a few lectures at Garrity University. Sometimes, life just gets in the way."

"Yeah, but your excuses were probably like 'my car won't start' or 'my mom called and I couldn't get off the phone because my aunt is in the hospital,'" Mia replied. "I don't think Zelda would accept 'I overslept because I stayed up too late hooking up with someone I probably shouldn't have.'"

"Bah, it'd be fine, she's not real anyways," Riley said, waving a dismissive hand.

Mia glanced over at her friend, taking in the confident set of her shoulders and the playful glint in her eyes. As an associate professor at the local university, Riley had managed to strike a balance between her professional life and her penchant for late-night whiskey-fueled adventures. She'd been involuntarily thrust into Mia's world a year ago, and had acclimated to it far easier than Mia had ever expected. When they met, they were both trying to rebuild their lives, and circumstances had pushed them together.

They were an unlikely pair, but Mia didn't think she'd still be here without Riley.

They rounded a corner, the quaint façade of the esoteric bookstore coming into view. Tucked between a florist's shop and a bakery, the century-old building exuded an air of mystery that seemed to seep from its walls. A simple sign saying "Markov Books" hung over the door.

As Mia unlocked the entrance, its dark red brick exterior gave way to a dimly lit interior filled with the scent of book paper and dust. Shelves upon shelves of books lined the walls, an odd mix of mass produced Llewelyn books and rare tomes that might actually contain something of significance. For every object of power in the store, there were twenty crystals and five random tarot decks that would appeal to a college kid or bored housewife. The strange dichotomy drew Mia in like a moth to a flame.

"This place sure does define the word 'eclectic,'" Riley remarked, her voice tinged with laughter.

Mia nodded in agreement. "Wouldn't have it any other way."

Zelda Markov, the elusive owner of the bookshop, had about a million rumors and stories told about her in town. Most of them weren't true, but she didn't remotely try to stop them. If anything she encouraged them because Zelda knew they were good for business.

"Have you seen Zelda recently?" Riley asked Mia quietly, their footsteps muffled by the worn and faded rugs that were scattered across the wooden floor.

"Not lately," Mia replied, peering down one of the shadowy aisles. "But you know how she is – always popping up when you least expect it."

"No, I don't know," Riley replied. "Because I've never actually *seen* her. I'm half convinced you and half the town made her up."

"She's a real person, Riley," Mia laughed. "I've met her multiple times. Her signature is on my paychecks."

"Nah, I don't believe you," Riley smiled. "Zelda Markov is like Ronald McDonald – or Wendy from Wendy's."

"Wendy's is named after a real person, Riley," Mia replied. "The founder named it after his daughter I think?"

"Poppycock," Mia said with a wink.

Mia was never sure whether or not this whole "Zelda isn't real" thing was serious or if Riley was just doing a bit. She was definitely committed to it if it was the latter.

As they continued to the back room so she could clock in, Mia spotted a copy of *Mugdow's Demonology*. Mia couldn't help but feel a reminder of the past she left behind when she came here. The guilt wasn't as constant as it was when she first arrived, but the dreams about what happened to Sarah in that warehouse in Boston hadn't stopped.

That night where Mia's recklessness almost destroyed the life of the only woman she'd ever truly loved.

"Hey, you've got that face," Riley said, placing a hand on Mia's shoulder, "I don't know *why* you have that face, but you have that face. If you need to talk, I'm here. I can stick around a bit longer."

"No, I'm fine," Mia paused for a moment. "It's just that yesterday marked two years since Sarah burned away half of her soul to save me. Two years since I caused so much pain. It's just fucking me up this morning. I'll be okay."

"Jesus, I had no idea," Riley replied. "I can cancel my classes and sit with you if you need me to."

"No, go. If I paused my life every time I got lost in regret, I'd never get anything done," Mia laughed. "Now you go off to your much better paying job and teach the future political wonks of America so I can start actually working."

"Doesn't pay *that* well, I don't have tenure, and pretty sure all of my freshmen are just there for the GE credit,"

Riley said with a bow, exiting the store. "I am coming by when I'm done for the day, and we are going to go have fun. I'm going to revive 'fun-Mia' if it kills me."

"Deal," Mia smiled.

The bell over the door jingled as it closed behind Riley.

Mia inhaled deeply, savoring the familiar scent of book-paper. As she made her way behind the counter, she went to adjust the crystals displayed there. They were largely paperweights and highly overpriced, but they kept the store in business as far as Mia could tell.

Not that Zelda ever let Mia see the accounts.

The morning flew by, with only a few people coming in. There were usually very few customers before the afternoon, but it gave Mia the opportunity to unload the latest stock shipments that had arrived the night before.

Because *of course* Mike hadn't done it himself.

Mike was technically the store manager, but Mia was never sure what he actually did beyond read the paper and tell Mia what to do. Mike was, quite literally, the most boring person ever to grace the world with his presence.

Long after the day shifted into late afternoon, while absentmindedly placing books back on the shelf, Mia found herself staring at the books on demonology again. A particularly worn and dog-eared book loomed on the shelf, its spine cracked from years of use. It was a guide to demonic possession - a copy of the same one she had read obsessively during her darkest days. The vivid memories of the sensations she experienced while under the influence of malevolent beings still haunted her: the searing heat coursing through her veins, her heart pounding like a war drum while the demon whispered sweet nothings into her thoughts. The ecstasy that shook her body as she took control of an otherworldly being...

"Hey, Mia!" a cheery voice called out, snapping her back to reality. A young woman with vibrant purple hair and an array of piercings entered the bookstore, her eyes wide with excitement. "Is that tarot deck I ordered in?"

"Not yet Nic, we got an email from the publisher saying they're having an issue with their printers," Mia replied cheerfully, pushing aside her dark memories to focus on the present moment. "Sorry about that."

"That sucks," Nic said, her fingers fidgeting excitedly. "The illustrations are absolutely stunning. I can't wait to do a reading with it. It's been two and a half weeks though."

"Yeah, but them's the breaks, kid. It gets like this with independent publishers some times," Mia agreed. Mia liked Nic. Nic worked at the nearby record store, and had checked in on that order at least three times in the last week. "I promise to personally text you when we get any updates though."

"Thanks, Mia. You're the best," Nic said, her gratitude evident in her warm expression.

"Of course, anytime." Mia watched as Nic browsed a nearby shelf. Nic was always so adorable, and reminded Mia of herself when she was much more innocent.

"Hey, Mia?" Nic held up a book on exorcisms, her eyebrows raised in curiosity. "What do you think about this one? Is it worth a read?"

"It's by Craig Lovekins..." Mia hesitated for a moment, the subject matter hitting too close to home for a moment. "It's super bad, and I'd recommend another book instead. There's one called 'The Light Within the Shadows' – it delves into various methods of spiritual cleansing and protection. I think you'll find it way more useful, and not full of Margaret Murray bullshit."

"Alright, solid call," Nic said, returning the exorcism book to the shelf and picking up Mia's suggestion.

"Thank you," Mia replied, having hopefully saved another customer from a shitty, shitty book.

The bell above the door chimed signaling Riley's return to the bookstore, her long blonde hair swinging with each confident step. "Don't teach intro classes to freshmen, they are the worst," Riley greeted Mia with a mild grimace.

"Yeah, I'll try to remember that if I ever get drunk and accidentally get multiple post-graduate degrees some weekend," Mia laughed. "Rough day?"

"The roughest," Riley sighed, concern etching itself onto her features. "Remind me why I became a professor?"

"Because you're terrified of exiting academia and finding out what the real world is like?" Mia smiled, her gaze darting to Nic who was now engrossed in her new book.

"That is... probably true," Riley replied. "How late are you working today? I want to get very, very drunk with you and watch you struggle to not answer Bobbi's texts for shits and giggles."

"My love life is not a spectator sport," Mia said with a smirk. "I'm not working much longer. Mike should be in to take over the shop in like fifteen minutes."

"Perfect," Riley smiled. "Then we can stop by your place, you can shower, and we can head out to the bars."

As they exited the bookstore together twenty minutes later, arm in arm, the sun cast long shadows on the streets of Parrish Mills. The town seemed to hold its breath, an unsettling stillness settling over the quaint storefronts and old brick walls. Mia's instincts prickled at the edges of her consciousness – something felt wrong, like a storm was coming on the horizon.

It was probably nothing.

Mia reminded herself not to be so paranoid.

Chapter 2

The night air was cold on Mia's skin as she pressed her body against Gina's, the warmth of their shared breath mingling with the faint scent of damp brick. Her lips found the young brunette's in an urgent dance, tongues exploring one another in a passionate tango that seemed to defy the passage of time.

"I like the way you taste," Gina murmured, her hands grasping at Mia's slender waist, fingers digging into her flesh just enough to elicit a gasp of pleasure. The sensation sent shivers down Mia's spine.

"Let's see how much more you like," Mia whispered, her voice barely audible over the distant hum of streetlights and traffic. She guided Gina's hand upward, past the curve of her breast, until her fingers rested on the thudding pulse of her neck. In that moment, Mia felt a flicker of vulnerability – a reminder that despite all her defenses, there were still parts of her that longed for connection, for trust.

And it was easier to escape the memories that were plaguing her today when she had a distraction.

As they kissed again, Mia could feel the rough texture of the alley wall grinding against her back, its coldness contrasting sharply with the heat radiating from Gina's body. Emboldened by desire, she hoisted herself up onto a nearby window sill, wrapping her legs around Gina's hips and pulling her closer. The press of their bodies, the friction of their movements, set every nerve in Mia's body alight with anticipation.

"God, you're amazing," Gina breathed, her voice ragged with lust. She trailed her lips down Mia's throat, teeth grazing lightly before nipping at her collarbone, sending a jolt of excitement straight to Mia's core.

In that instant, as Mia tilted her head back to allow Gina greater access to her sensitive skin, her eyes caught sight of something lying in the shadows beyond them. A man's body, pale and lifeless, with dark rivulets of blood pooling beneath it.

"Shit," Mia hissed under her breath, the sudden intrusion of reality shattering the erotic haze that had enveloped her. "Gina, look…"

With a gasp, Gina followed Mia's gaze. She stumbled back, her eyes wide with shock as they took in the gruesome scene before them. The dead body lay twisted at an unnatural angle, its glassy-eyed stare fixed eternally on the unforgiving night sky above.

"Who… what happened?" Gina stammered, her hands shaking as she clung to Mia for support.

Panic spread across Gina's face, her chest heaving as she struggled to catch her breath. "I can't… I have to go," she choked out, her voice trembling with fear. She tore herself from Mia's grasp and sprinted away down the alley, leaving Mia alone with the lifeless body.

"Shit," Mia muttered, her hands shaking as she pulled out her ancient flip phone. Her fingers fumbled on the keys, tapping out a frantic message to Riley: *need u. dead body in alley behind the bar. hurry!*

The cold of the autumn night seemed to finally hit Mia, the chill sinking into her bones as her adrenaline began to wane. Her tattoos seemed to pulsate beneath her flesh, almost flashing like a warning. The alley was silent now, save for the distant echo of sirens and laughter from the bars nearby.

This was not her first dead body, but it had been years since she was this close to a fresh one. At least she was sure this one wasn't her fault.

"Damn it, Mia," she whispered to herself, her eyes never leaving the gruesome sight before her. "Why can't you just have a normal night out?"

"Normal isn't really our thing, is it?" came a familiar voice, tinged with concern. Riley appeared at the entrance of the alley, her figure backlit by the neon lights of the neighboring bar. She strode forward purposefully, her eyes surveying the scene with composure despite the horror that lay before them. "I leave you alone for twenty minutes and you immediately find a corpse."

"Glad you're taking it well," Mia breathed, relief washing over her like a warm wave. "Because this is going to be a whole thing."

"First things first," Riley said, pulling her jacket off and draping it around Mia's shoulders. "Let's get you covered up. Secondly I'm taking this well because I'm *quite* drunk."

Riley crouched beside the body, examining it without touching. "You found him like this?"

Mia nodded, grateful for the protective warmth of the jacket as she shivered. "Yeah. Gina and I were… well, we were having fun, and then I saw him."

"Where's Gina now?" Riley asked, her eyes flicking up to meet Mia's.

"She freaked out and ran," Mia admitted. "I don't blame her. This is a far cry from teaching kindergarten."

"Yeah, and the school board might want an explanation if she ended up on the news," Riley sighed, standing up and placing a comforting hand on Mia's shoulder. "Alright, we need to call the police. This isn't something we should try to handle on our own."

Mia hesitated, her thoughts racing with the implications of their discovery. She didn't like cops. Mia had very, very *bad* experiences with cops. She swallowed hard, pushing aside her her own baggage. It would certainly look worse for her if they *didn't* call the cops.

"Okay," she agreed softly. "Let's do what we have to do."

Mia's heart pounded in her chest, a relentless drum that mirrored the intensity of Riley's gaze as she scrutinized the body before them. In the dim streetlight the dead man's body had an almost ethereal quality.

"Look at his neck," Riley murmured, her whiskey-laden breath ghosting over Mia's cheek. "Those two holes – they're like a bite mark out of a cheesy vampire movie."

A shiver ran down Mia's spine as she observed the strange puncture wounds. One of the sigils on the back of her neck seemed to hum with energy, letting her know something was up. She glanced nervously at Riley, whose eyes flitted between the corpse and the near-empty street, a mixture of fear and deep thought hanging on her face.

"Riley, you should be the one to call," Mia said quietly. "I just… I just can't handle it right now."

"Agreed," Riley replied, pulling out her phone and dialing 911. As she spoke with the dispatcher, Mia's thoughts spiraled into a vortex of panic and self-doubt. She knew this wasn't her fault, but it was triggering memories of the last time she stood over a lifeless body.

That time it *had* been her fault.

"Police are on their way," Riley said, hanging up and pocketing her phone. Her hand found Mia's, giving it a reassuring squeeze. "We did the right thing."

"I hope so." Mia sighed, her breath fogging in the chilly air. *Riley's right – it does look like a vampire movie... and we definitely aren't in a movie. Most vampires wouldn't be this sloppy.*

Mia leaned on Riley, and the two stood there in silence. As they waited for the police, Mia's sigils seemed to quiet down, as if whatever energy had been here was fading.

After some time, the wail of approaching sirens pierced the night, their red and blue lights casting strange shades on the brick walls. The police cars stopped at the mouth of the alley, and uniformed officers disembarked, their boots crunching on the gravel as they approached.

"Stay behind me," Riley whispered, stepping protectively in front of Mia. Their breaths mingled in the cold air, leaving ghostly trails that vanished just as quickly as they appeared.

"Evening, ladies," one officer said, his voice gruff but not unkind. "I'm Officer Daniels, and this is my partner, Officer Thompson. We received a call about a body?"

"Yes," Mia said calmly, her gaze flickering between the two men. "It's over there," she added, pointing towards the corpse. Mia was actually a little thankful she was reacting to this far more severely than normal. If she was fully herself, she'd probably put on a calm face instinctively. Too calm. It'd probably make her look significantly more suspicious to the cops.

Hooray for convenient trauma, Mia thought internally, not sure if she wanted to cry about it or just sigh. As the officers moved past them to examine the body, Mia couldn't help but overhear their hushed conversation.

"Damn, another one," Officer Thompson muttered, his brow furrowed in concern. "This makes three this month."

"Same MO, too," Officer Daniels agreed, his eyes narrowing as he studied the bite marks on the victim's neck. "We've got a serial killer on our hands."

Mia's heart clenched at their words, her stomach twisting into knots. *Three bodies?* she thought, fear wrapping icy tendrils around her spine. The dead man had tripped her supernatural alarms, and if it wasn't the only one... *We are so fucked.*

"Ma'am, can you tell us what happened?" Officer Daniels asked, snapping Mia out of her thoughts.

"Uh, we...we found the body like this," Mia replied, her voice barely audible. She was doing such a good job sounding like the scared young woman shocked by death the cops would expect. Mia tried to convince herself it was just an act.

"Did either of you see anything suspicious? Anyone leaving the scene?" Officer Thompson inquired, his expression serious.

"Nothing," Riley said firmly, her words laced with a hint of frustration. "We got here, and the body was already like this."

"Alright then," Officer Daniels sighed, rubbing the back of his neck. "We're going to need both of you to come down to the station to give a statement. It's just protocol."

"Of course," Mia agreed, her mind racing. In theory the spell to keep the police from identifying her with her past criminal record should be working, but she had never tested it before. *This will be fine. It has to be fine.*

She and Riley climbed into the back of the police car as the ambulance arrived. Mia's tattoos seemed to pulse beneath her skin, a reminder that no matter how far she ran, the darkness at the edge of the world was never far behind.

Chapter 3

Mia's apartment felt like a refuge after a draining three hours spent talking to the police. The dim light from Mia's single lamp cast long shadows on the walls, and the scent of stale unwashed laundry provided a strange sense of comfort that had been missing the entire night. Grabbing a bottle from the top of Mia's fridge, Riley sank into the old battered couch, her exhaustion evident in the way her body seemed to fold in on itself.

"Jesus, Mia," Riley breathed out, running a hand through her disheveled hair. "I can't believe we found a freakin' body." Her whiskey-tinged voice was thick with disbelief and horror.

Mia paced back and forth across the room, her stress-sweat making her tattoos appear to shine under the dim light. She wrung her hands together, her anxiety palpable. "Riley, there's something I need to tell you."

"Of course there is." Riley took a swig from the bottle, savoring the burn as it slid down her throat, offering a temporary reprieve from the reality they were facing.

"You joked about it in the alley, but vampires are actually real."

Riley choked on her whiskey, eyes watering as she tried to find her breath. "What?!" she managed to gasp out once she regained her composure. "I thought you were the sober one here, Mia."

"Oh I definitely feel like I should be drinking," Mia muttered under her breath. She stopped pacing and looked Riley directly in the eye, her expression serious. "I'm not joking, Riles. Vampires are real, and this town is home to at least one that I know about."

"You waited until now to tell me that vampires exist?" Riley said, leaning forward. "I mean, I feel like that's pertinent information."

"It never came up!" Mia shrugged. "How exactly was I supposed to just slip that in! Like, it's not something that comes up in conversation, and I didn't know how you would handle it."

"I live in a haunted house," Riley returned. "I feel like I'm pretty open minded."

"There's a difference between dead-kid Gertie who hides your sugar and the fanged undead," Mia replied quietly.

"Okay, okay," Riley said, holding up a hand to stop Mia. "You're forgiven. This vampire you know in town, do they go around killing people? Like the body we found?"

"Most vampires don't kill humans," Mia explained, her voice steady despite the bizarre nature of their conversation. "They've learned to control their thirst and live alongside us, taking only what they need and leaving the rest. Fuck, most do it consensually. It's a whole kink thing."

"Then why are you telling me this, Mia?" Riley asked, her brow furrowed in confusion. "If the vampire you've met here wouldn't do this..."

"Because," Mia replied, a hint of fear creeping into her voice, "Maybe there's one around I *don't* know. And if one did kill that guy, we're all in danger."

"Point taken," Riley said, nodding. After taking a deep breath, Riley spoke again, "So what vampire *does* live in town?"

"Her name's Lucy Vitale," Mia said, fingers nervously tapping against her thigh. "She lives in an old Victorian house at the edge of town near the river. I've spent some time with her."

"Lucy Vitale," Riley echoed, she started to look at Mia suspiciously, like she was putting something together slowly. "How long is 'some time,' like how well do you actually know her."

"Pretty well? I think?" Mia replied. Her gaze drifted toward the window as she continued, "I first met her like six months ago? If I'm confident of anything, it's that she hasn't hurt or killed anyone."

The gears finished turning in Riley's head.

"Oh god you've slept with her," she sighed, rubbing her temples. "You one hundred percent slept with a vampire."

"Just once!" Mia sighed.

"Ghosts and Vampires..." Riley said quietly to herself. "Is there a supernatural creature you won't hook up with?"

"Gnomes," Mia said, putting on a mock serious voice. "Not remotely into Gnomes."

"What, the little pointy hats don't do it for you?" Riley laughed. "So, what's the plan? We go to this Lucy person and ask her if she knows anything about the dead bodies?"

"More or less," Mia confirmed with a nod. "I just want some answers. I don't think she's involved, but maybe she can help us figure out who is. I assume vampires talk to each other."

"An assumption," Riley sighed. "We're going off of an assumption. At two in the morning. Wait, is everything you know about vampires from a random hookup you had?"

"Do you have a better idea?"

"Fine," Riley conceded, taking one last swig of whiskey before setting the bottle down on the side table. "Let's go talk to a vampire. You're driving though."

"Obviously."

The two made their way to Mia's old rusty pickup truck, which very much looked like it had seen better days. As they climbed inside, the aged leather seats creaked beneath them, a testament to the years of use.

"Going to see a vampire in this thing?" Riley teased, running her fingers along a jagged tear in the upholstery. "Real inconspicuous. No one will notice the exhaust rattle as we drive down their street in the middle of the night, I'm sure."

"Hey, it gets us where we need to go," Mia retorted playfully, turning the key in the ignition. The engine roared to life, a familiar symphony of clanks, shaking, and hums that comforted Mia, even in this tense situation. "Also, it's not my fault you left your car over by the bar."

As they drove through the quiet streets of Parrish Mills, Mia could sense Riley's building sense of foreboding. She'd only met Riley a year ago, and already had to introduce her to the idea that magic and ghosts and other spooky things were real.

But now Riley was finding out about the *real* monsters.

"Hey, you okay?" Mia asked, noticing Riley's distant expression. "I thought I was the one falling apart tonight."

"I'm fine," Riley said quietly, putting a noticeably forced smile on her face. "Just sobering up a bit and trying to wrap my head around all of this."

"Trust me, Riley, so am I," Mia admitted, her eyes fixed on the road ahead. The further they ventured from the center of town, the more isolated their surroundings became. Tall trees loomed over the narrow street, their gnarled branches reaching out like skeletal fingers.

"Almost there," Mia whispered, as if afraid to disturb the heavy silence that had fallen between them.

Finally, the outline of an old Victorian house appeared in the distance, its turrets and gables a stark contrast against the dark sky. It wasn't as large as Riley's infamous home, but was certainly just as old.

"Ready for this?" Mia asked, turning off the engine and meeting Riley's gaze with a mix of determination and fear.

"Ready as I'll ever be," Riley replied, her voice barely above a whisper. Together, they stepped out of the truck and made their way toward the imposing residence.

The wind sighed through the leafless branches, as if the trees themselves were mourning the loss of summer's warmth. The air was thick with tension as Mia approached the house, with Riley close behind. Each step closer to the looming structure seemed to steal the breath from her lungs, her tattoos pulsating against her skin like a living, writhing force.

She could feel the supernatural essence threaded throughout the property.

"Maybe we should have called ahead," Riley muttered, her eyes darting from the cracked windows to the peeling paint of the door.

"Lucy doesn't have a phone – or at least that's what she told me last we talked," Mia replied with certainty, her voice barely audible amidst the eerie whispers of the wind. She raised her hand and knocked firmly on the door, her knuckles striking the weathered wood like a judge's gavel demanding order.

For several heartbeats, there was nothing but the creaking of the house and the rustling of leaves. Then, the door slowly inched open, revealing a sliver of Lucy's face. Her eyes, dark and impenetrable, bore into Mia's with an intensity that sent shivers down her spine.

"Leave," Lucy hissed, her voice the very essence of temptation and danger. "You shouldn't be here."

"Lucy, please," Mia implored, desperation seeping into her tone. "We need your help."

"Go!" Lucy snarled, her fangs glinting in the dim light.

"Hi, Lucy? I'm Riley," Riley interjected boldly, her whiskey-honed courage rising to the surface. "Someone's been killed. We need to know if a vampire did it."

A flicker of something – regret? concern? – passed across Lucy's face before she finally relented. With a slow, deliberate movement, she opened the door wider and stepped aside, allowing Mia and Riley entry into her home.

"Emma!" she called out, her voice sharp as a whip. "Get to the basement. Now."

A young woman with a short neon red pixie cut and wild eyes appeared from a shadowy corner, her gaze locked onto Mia and Riley like a predator sizing up its prey. "But, Lucy–" she began.

"Go!" Lucy commanded again, her voice brooking no argument. Emma's shoulders slumped in defeat as she turned and hurried down a narrow corridor, disappearing from sight.

"Basement?" Riley asked, her bravado faltering slightly as she eyed the darkness that swallowed Emma whole.

"Emma is still mastering herself," Lucy replied coldly, her eyes never leaving Mia's. "Now tell me what you want, witch."

"Who's the girl?" Mia's heart pounded in her chest, the steady thrum of blood through her veins an unwelcome reminder of her vulnerability. Lucy's gaze was predatory, her eyes seemingly taking the entirety of Mia in as she spoke.

Lucy was shorter than Mia, but she *seemed* taller. She was beautiful, her long black hair plaited and held up with a hairpin decorated with roses. She wore a long black skirt and a simple top, but it clung to her perfect curves. Lucy was probably the most beautiful woman Mia had ever seen, and Mia could tell Riley was just as entranced.

"Emma is…new," Lucy began hesitantly, her voice a sultry purr that sent shivers down Mia's spine. "Her control is not what it should be. I've taken it upon myself to train her."

"Train her?" Riley scoffed, arching an eyebrow as she clutched her whiskey flask for comfort. "From what we've seen, someone out there has got a taste for blood, and you just said she doesn't have control. The cops have found multiple bodies with vampire bites on them."

"Riley!" Mia admonished, her eyes darting between her friend and the dangerous vampire before them. Maybe bringing a drunk person to a potentially deadly supernatural creature was a *bad* idea.

"Enough," Lucy snapped, her patience wearing thin. "You came here seeking answers. I assure you, Emma has not left this house."

A sudden thud from upstairs echoed through the room, followed by a muffled whimper. Riley's attention immediately snapped upward, her instincts honed by years of academia and suspicion. "What was that?"

"Nothing you need concern yourself with," Lucy replied a bit too quickly, her eyes narrowing as she assessed the situation.

"Like hell it isn't!" Riley retorted, her grip tightening into a fist. "If there's someone else up there, we need to know!"

"Riley, please," Mia pleaded softly, placing a hand on her friend's arm. But Riley remained steadfast, her eyes locked on Lucy as she awaited an explanation. Lucy was beautiful, but so was a tiger – and Mia definitely didn't want to see Riley get eaten.

"Fine fine," Lucy finally relented, her lips pulling back into a tight smile that revealed her sharp fangs. "Come. You'll see there is nothing wrong here."

As they ascended the creaking staircase, Mia couldn't help but feel a growing sense of unease. She knew in her bones that something was off, but she couldn't put her finger on it. The darkness seemed to close in around them, threatening to smother Mia's resolve.

"Who's up there?" Riley demanded again as they reached the top of the stairs, her voice steady despite the fear gnawing at her gut.

"Patience, child," Lucy chided, her voice dripping with sarcasm. "All will be revealed."

Mia closed her eyes for a moment, trying to calm her racing thoughts. She had come here seeking answers, but now she wasn't sure she wanted to know the truth.

Lucy unlocked a hidden door, revealing a set of stairs up to an attic, and the three began to ascend.

The air in the attic was heavy with the scent of aged wood and a hint of something sweet. Mia's eyes took a moment to adjust to the dim lights that illuminated the space. The space they found themselves in looked far more like a luxurious boudoir than an attic.

It was frankly far larger and nicer than Mia's apartment.

"Jayla," Lucy called out smoothly, her voice echoing through the room. A figure emerged from the shadows, a lithe young woman wearing a crimson silk robe that hung loosely around her delicate frame. Her dark hair cascaded over her shoulders, framing a face that held a serene, otherworldly beauty.

"Ah, Mistress," the young woman breathed, dropping to her knees before Lucy. "You've brought guests."

"Jesus Christ, Jayla – please just get up and act normally," Lucy said quietly pinching the bridge of her nose. There was a note of warmth in her voice that Mia hadn't heard before. As Jayla stood, her gaze flicked towards Mia and Riley, her expression unreadable. Mia felt a shiver race down her spine at the intensity of those eyes.

"Jayla is under my protection," Lucy explained, her fingers brushing against the nape of Jayla's neck in a gesture both possessive and tender. "She lives here willingly."

"Protection from what?" Riley asked, her brow furrowed in confusion.

"From the world outside, and these days also from Emma," Jayla replied softly, her voice barely above a whisper. "I feel safe up here, away from the chaos outside."

"Jayla is a mortal human," Lucy explained. "We met five years ago, and I took her in."

As she spoke, Mia couldn't help but notice the way Jayla's eyes lingered on Lucy, a mixture of longing and adoration in her gaze. It was clear that the bond between the two women ran deep, deeper than any conventional relationship.

And something about it seemed kind of fucked up.

"Emma can't come up here?" Mia inquired, trying to understand the dynamics at play.

"Correct," Lucy confirmed, her gaze never leaving Jayla. "This is Jayla's sanctuary, her place of safety. Emma is not permitted to enter."

"Besides," Jayla added with a wry smile, "Even if she could get past all the locks, I doubt she would dare to defy my Mistress."

"Stop referring to me as that," Lucy said quietly. "This is… this is serious Jayla."

"Oh, but I wouldn't want to defy my Mistress," Jayla said in almost a mock deference.

"I'm not kidding, they're going to get the wrong idea," Lucy whispered emphatically. "Just be your normal self?"

"Oh fine, take the fun out of it," Jayla replied, crossing her arms.

The air crackled with tension as Mia processed what exactly was happening in front of her.

"Is there anything else you need to know?" Lucy asked, her voice laced with impatience.

"I mean, I have a *lot* of questions, but none of them related to why we're here," Riley said quietly.

"Let's get back to the matter at hand," Mia said quietly, "There's clearly a vampire in town wreaking havoc, and we need assurances it's not coming from you."

"What assurances could I possibly give?" Lucy asked. "It's strange, you seemed to trust me the last time we met, Mia."

"It's not… look. I just found out Emma existed, and she looked pretty hungry to me," Mia replied. "You say she hasn't left the house, but how do I know that? How do *you* know that?"

"I think I can answer that," Jayla chimed in, gesturing for everyone to follow her. As Jayla led them through the space, her fingers trailed delicately along a row of monitors that lined one wall.

"Here," she murmured, brushing her fingertips against the screen as images flickered to life. "These are feeds from every room in the house, as well as the surrounding yard. I feel more secure knowing what's going on in the rest of the house, and Lucy indulges me."

Riley leaned in closer, scrutinizing the screens with furrowed brows. "There – the basement," she said, pointing at one of the monitors. A grainy image revealed Emma pacing back and forth, occasionally glancing at the camera.

"See?" Lucy purred, sidling up to Mia. Her voice was like velvet, rich and smooth, sending a shiver down Mia's spine. "Emma hasn't set foot outside of this house since the night we brought her here."

Mia's pulse quickened at Lucy's proximity, her breath catching in her throat as their eyes met. She felt the vampire's cool fingers brush against her wrist, tracing the outline of a rune tattoo, and struggled to suppress the urge to lean into her touch.

People respond to stressful situations in different ways, and it occurred to Mia that *maybe* hers weren't the healthiest.

"Your sigils..." Lucy whispered, her lips a hair's breadth from Mia's earlobe. "They're beautiful, just like you. It's fascinating, Because of that one on your left shoulder I couldn't feed off of you even if you wanted me to."

"My desires lie elsewhere than being fed on," Mia said with a smirk.

"Uh, guys?" Riley interrupted, dragging her eyes away from the monitor. "As much as I hate to break up whatever's happening here, we should probably keep focus for like an entire five minutes?"

Jayla just smirked and shook her head.

"Right," Mia agreed, tearing her gaze from Lucy's hypnotic eyes. She took a step back, acutely aware of the heat that radiated from her own body, contrasting sharply with the chill of the vampire's touch. "We need to figure out what happened to that body we found."

"Very well," Lucy sighed, disappointment flickering across her features before she resumed her usual stoic demeanor. "But rest assured, my dear Mia, Emma is not responsible for that unfortunate incident."

"Then who is?" Riley demanded, frustration evident in her voice.

"Do you know of any other vampires in town, Lucy?" Mia asked.

"No, I do not," Lucy said shaking her head.

Mia sat there for a moment, trying to figure out what to do next, when the blindingly obvious struck her.

"Wait. When we first met, you told me you swore not to turn anyone, Lucy," Mia said quietly. "Where the hell did Emma come from?"

The room hung in silence, the tension almost palpable.

"Emma..." Lucy hesitated, her voice a breathy whisper. "I don't know where she came from. The night I found her, she was covered in blood, her memory of that night lost to the shadows."

"And you didn't think it was pertinent to mention that?" Mia asked, slightly shocked.

"The blood was her own," Lucy sighed. "Mixed with that of a wild animal's. There was no trace of another human on her at all."

Mia's tattoos tingled beneath her clothes, reacting to the supernatural energy that seemed to radiate from Lucy's very being. She bit her lip, torn between curiosity and caution. "I need to speak to her. See if I can find out what happened."

Lucy's eyes narrowed, her sensuous lips curled into a frown. "I'm not sure that's a good idea, Mia. Emma is... unpredictable."

"Trust me," Mia urged, gripping the edge of the antique table they stood beside. "I've dealt with worse things than a young vampire. Besides, it's not like she can feed on me, right?"

For a moment, Lucy hesitated, her gaze lingering on Mia's tattoos as if evaluating the truth of her words. Finally, she sighed, her delicate shoulders sagging under the weight of her decision. "Very well. But do not say I didn't warn you."

Lucy guided Mia down through the house, eventually arriving at the basement stairs. As they descended, Mia could feel the temperature drop with each step, the dampness seeping into her bones. She shivered, rubbing her arms to ward off the chill, but the cold seemed to cling to her like a lover's touch.

The basement door creaked open, revealing a dimly lit space filled with shadows that danced along the stone walls. In the center of the room, a figure huddled on the floor.

Emma.

"Emma," Lucy called out softly, her voice laced with concern. "Mia is here to speak with you. She thinks she may be able to help."

The girl looked up, her eyes almost like a wild animal. There was a rage and hunger there, something deeply seeded. She was like a caged animal longing for freedom.

"Remember what I've taught you," Lucy whispered, giving Mia one last warning glance before leaving them alone in the cold darkness of the basement.

As Mia approached Emma, she couldn't help but wonder if she'd made the right decision. This girl might have layers of trauma that went far beyond the night she was turned.

"Alright, Emma," Mia said, her voice steady despite the unease churning in her stomach like a nest of snakes. The danger was intoxicating, though Mia would never admit it. "We're alone now. You can talk to me."

Emma remained huddled on the floor, her pale skin almost luminescent in the candlelight. Her shoulders shook, and Mia couldn't tell if it was from fear or anger. She took a cautious step closer, watching Emma closely for any signs of sudden movement.

"Emma, I'm here to help you," Mia said softly, trying to establish a connection. "I know you can't remember what happened the night you were turned, but I might be able to–"

In an instant, Emma lunged at Mia, her face contorted into a snarl, fangs bared. Caught off guard by the sudden attack, Mia stumbled backward, tripping over her own feet and landing hard on the cold stone floor. A sharp pain shot up her spine, but she didn't have time to dwell on it, focusing instead on the predator hovering above her.

"You can't help me!" Emma hissed, her eyes wild with fear and rage. "I'm this thing now, and there's no changing that."

Mia forced herself to remain calm, her heart thundering in her chest like a thrash metal drummer with a double bass pedal. This was not the time for panic. She had to reach Emma, to actually get this girl to trust her.

"Emma, listen to me," Mia said, her voice firm yet gentle. "I know you're scared, and I understand why. But I'm not here to hurt you. I want to help you find the truth about what happened."

As she spoke, Mia could feel the powerful energy of her tattoos pulsing beneath her skin, defensive spells activating instinctively. She knew in her head that Emma wouldn't be able to hurt her *too* much – not with the protection the sigils provided – but getting her stomach on board was a tougher sell.

"Please," Mia whispered, staring into Emma's eyes. "Trust me."

For a moment, it seemed as if Emma might relent. Her snarl softened, and something like hope flickered in her eyes. But then, just as quickly, her expression hardened once more, and she pressed her advantage, pinning Mia to the ground with surprising strength.

"Leave me alone," Emma spat, her breath hot against Mia's face. "Or I'll make you wish you had."

Behind the anger and the threat, Mia could sense the pain that drove Emma – the fear of the unknown, the terror of her own power. She almost felt a kinship with this girl, thinking about how terrifying it had been when she entered this world herself. And unlike Mia, Emma couldn't choose to leave it if she wanted.

"Emma," Mia said softly, feeling the cold stone pressing against her back. "You don't have to do this. Let me help you."

It occurred to Mia that under other circumstances being pinned to the ground by an athletic young woman was her idea of a good time, and it was really becoming difficult not to laugh about it.

Laughing would definitely not help.

Emma's fangs grazed Mia's throat, the sharp tips biting into her skin but not quite breaking it. The sensation was almost sensual. Confusion clouded Emma's predatory gaze as she tried to sink her teeth deeper though, only to be met with an invisible barrier.

"You know, most girls would buy me a drink first," Mia taunted, her voice breathless but steady. She smirked up at the vampire straddling her. "Maybe get to know me a bit before going straight to any kind of penetration."

Emma snarled in frustration, tightening her grip on Mia's wrists, but the sigils etched into her skin continued to protect her from harm. The air between them crackled with tension, charged by their respective powers. Emma tried to bite Mia again, and it kind of tickled.

"I mean, I'm not against a little roughness in foreplay, but maybe we should set a safeword," Mia teased, flexing her fingers against the cold, unforgiving stone floor. A flicker of amusement danced in her eyes, even as her heart hammered wildly in her chest. "Maybe something like 'Apple' or 'Red.'"

"Shut up!" Emma hissed, her face inches from Mia's. Their breaths mingled, warm and cool, human and supernatural.

"Make me," Mia dared, locking her gaze with Emma's, challenging the vampire to overcome the magic that shielded her. Mia was probably enjoying this more than she should.

****

In the attic, Riley found herself sitting cross-legged on the floor, facing Jayla as she lounged on the bed. The dim glow of of the monitors illuminated the space, giving the room a dim, blue glow. It made the space feel both oddly cold and intimate.

"Honestly, Lucy's great. She's taken care of me when I couldn't necessarily deal with things myself," Jayla said softly, her hands folded in her lap. "I never have to worry about going outside or dealing with people. It's just too... overwhelming."

"Are you saying you're agoraphobic?" Riley asked, curiosity piqued. She had never encountered someone who willingly lived in confinement, even with Lucy as a guardian.

"Never been diagnosed, but it wouldn't shock me. It was always… hard… but after 2020 it just kind of got way worse," Jayla admitted with a small shrug, her shoulders rising and falling gracefully. "And before you ask, yes I have a therapist. We do appointments online. But what I know is that when I'm out *there*, I feel like there's a steel cage closing around my chest and I can't breath. But here? Here, I feel safe."

"Safe" was not a word Riley would have used to describe living with a vampire, but she could understand the allure of sanctuary amidst the darkness. And as they sat there, trading stories in hushed voices, she found herself drawn to Jayla – not just her circumstances, but the woman herself.

"Strange," Riley mused, her thoughts momentarily turning inward. "I never thought I'd find someone who seemed so content in their own prison."

"Because it's not a prison at all. I control the locks," Jayla replied, her voice quite matter of fact. "Only thing keeping me up here is my own dumb brain. Lucy just does her best to make sure I'm comfortable."

The flickering light from a single candle on the the nightstand danced across Jayla's face, casting her features in a warm, golden glow. As she spoke with Riley, she seemed to settle into their conversation, her body language becoming more relaxed and inviting. Riley couldn't help but find herself liking the very strange woman.

"Please don't be offended, but you're speaking pretty differently than when we first showed up," Riley said. "You seemed like a different person."

"I mean, I like to play the role when Lucy's around, but I'm actually pretty normal," Jayla smiled, her demeanor relaxing. "I know it's easy to believe that I'm isolated here, but I'm not. I keep in touch with friends online, and I still talk to my family regularly."

Riley hesitated, weighing her words carefully before responding. "What does your family think about your... arrangement." She trailed off, trying to be tactful.

"They think I live with someone I'm seeing named Lucy," Jayla mused. "Which is true enough."

"Fair," Riley said, feeling a little more comfortable. "But I just honestly can't imagine being in a relationship where I'd be wholly reliant on someone else."

"Don't knock it till you try it," Jayla smiled, leaning back on the bed.

****

Emma sat cross-legged on the cold stone floor of the basement, watching Mia with a mixture of apprehension and curiosity. Emma had tried to feed from her for a good fifteen minutes before giving up. It was almost cute.

"Are you sure this will work?" Emma asked, her voice barely above a whisper.

"Nothing's for sure with this kind of magic no matter how many times you've done it," Mia replied, her fingers tracing patterns over her tattoos. "But it's worth a shot." Her breath hitched as she reached the final glyph, the air around them charged with an electric anticipation.

"Alright, here goes nothing," Mia murmured, pressing her palm against Emma's forehead. "Just a warning, this is probably going to suck."

At first, there was only darkness. Then, images began to flicker through Emma's mind like a film reel come to life. The night she was turned played out before her in vivid, startling detail. She relived the icy grip of fear as her attacker sunk their fangs into her neck, the searing pain that consumed her as her body writhed and convulsed. Her memories were jagged shards, cutting through the haze that had shrouded that night for too long.

"Stop!" Emma gasped, pulling away from Mia's touch, trembling with raw emotion.

"Did it work?" Mia asked, concern etched on her face.

"Y-yes," Emma stammered, tears streaming down her cheeks. "I remember everything."

"Good." Mia's voice was gentle, but firm. "What can you tell me about the vampire who turned you."

****

Mia ascended the creaking basement stairs, each step groaning beneath her as if protesting her departure. As she emerged into the hallway, the scent of stale air and ancient dust hung heavy in the atmosphere, clinging to the back of her throat like a stubborn cough.

"Lucy," Mia called out, her voice reverberating through the gloomy passageway. She could feel the lingering remnants of Emma's memories swirling around inside her head, threatening to overtake her own thoughts. It was like a bad hangover.

"Here," Lucy replied, appearing from the shadows with an ethereal grace that only centuries of vampiric existence could bestow. Her eyes, dark pools of curiosity and concern, bore into Mia's as she asked, "What happened? Did you find out anything?"

"Emma remembers everything – well, at least the night she was turned." Mia sighed, placing her hands on her hips. "But she never saw his face."

"But we know it was a man," Lucy replied. "That's more than we knew before."

"She knows where she was when she was turned too, and maybe this vampire has a hunting ground. It's possible he's the one leaving bodies around town." The words spilled from Mia's lips with a determination that belied her nerves, her heart pounding wildly within her chest.

"Or Emma's not the only one he's turned, and there are young, feral vampires running around this town," Lucy said, her brow furrowing with apprehension. "The danger could be greater than we believe."

"Maybe," Mia conceded, her resolve unwavering. "Which means we don't really have any choice but to try and stop it. Lucy, I could use your support." She locked eyes with Lucy, silently pleading for her agreement.

Lucy hesitated, weighing the potential risks against the tantalizing promise of a solution. Finally, she nodded, her expression a mixture of trepidation and determination. "Very well," she murmured, her voice barely audible over the hushed whispers of the house itself. "I'll do what I can."

"Thank you," Mia breathed. "It's the least you could do since you never called me back after that night six months ago."

"I literally do not own a phone, Mia," Lucy sighed.

"Excuses, excuses," Mia replied with a wink.

Chapter 4

Riley Whittaker stumbled through the heavy oak doors of Marshall Hall at Garrity University. Her eyes were bloodshot and once neat hair hastily tied back in a tangled ponytail. She instantly regretted her decision not to cancel her classes after the night she'd just experienced. The scent of whiskey clung to her like an unwanted companion, an annoying reminder of what a good idea going out had seemed the day before.

"Get it together, Riley," she muttered under her breath, trying to muster the strength to perform her duties as an associate professor. She clutched a stack of disorganized documents to her chest, feeling the weight of her exhaustion seeping into her deepest depths. Sleep and a shower probably would have helped, but at least she'd had a chance to change her clothes.

As she trudged down the hallway, the unsettling events from the night before played on repeat in her mind. She was not designed for all-nighters anymore, and the twenty minutes of sleep she *had* managed to sneak in left her feeling more tired than anything else

Damn it, Riley thought. *Why can't this just be someone else's problem? Why am I incapable of not making it mine?*

Lost in her thoughts, Riley rounded the corner and collided with a solid figure. The impact sent her documents flying like a flock of startled birds, scattering across the polished floor.

"Ah! I'm so sorry!" she blurted out, her cheeks flushing with embarrassment. She looked up to find the handsome new head of the History Department standing before her. Carson Smith's dark eyes held a magnetic intensity that seemed to pierce right through her.

"No harm done, Dr. Whittaker," Carson replied smoothly, his voice velvety and deep. A knowing smile danced on his lips as he studied her disheveled appearance. "You look like you could use a hand."

"Th-Thank you," Riley stammered, trying to ignore the electric shiver that ran down her spine as they both crouched down to gather the scattered papers. Their hands brushed against each other, and she couldn't help but notice how warm and strong his fingers were. Carson had only been with the university a few months, and Riley was genuinely surprised that he even knew her name.

Riley, focus, she scolded herself internally, acutely aware of Carson's magnetic presence. *You cannot be this pathetic*. It had been a fairly dry year for Riley, with only the occasional mistake since her ex- had dumped her weeks before their wedding. This was hardly the time to be thinking about climbing back on the horse.

Or on top of a history professor.

"Seems like I've made quite the mess here," she said, trying to stop from making too much of an ass of herself. She could feel Carson's eyes on her, taking in her disheveled appearance in. This was not the first impression she wanted to make.

"Indeed," Carson replied, his voice a low rumble that sent shivers down her spine. "But sometimes, chaos can give way to order – or even create new opportunities."

"True," Riley mused, looking up at him with a small smile. "I've always believed that a little disorder can be... enlightening." Their gazes locked, and for a moment, everything else faded away.

They finished gathering the papers, hands brushing once more before straightening up. The air between them was charged, and Riley couldn't help but imagine what it would be like to press her body against Carson's, to feel his strong arms wrapped around her. To feel his lips pressed against her neck. But reality came crashing back as she glanced at the clock on the wall.

If she didn't get moving now, she was going to be late.

"I need to get going. Thank you... again," Riley managed, said, attempting to regain her composure. With a forced laugh, she added, "I guess I should watch where I'm going next time."

"Perhaps," Carson agreed, his smile enigmatic. "But some collisions are worth the trouble."

With that, he strode off down the hallway, leaving Riley breathless and unnerved. She clutched the documents to her chest once more, her mind racing. *Dear lord, what am I, a teenager? I don't think I could be more pathetic if I tried right now.*

Heading into the lecture hall, Riley tried to focus on teaching her classes, but her thoughts were consumed by Carson. She replayed their encounter over and over, imagining different scenarios in which she had been bolder, more daring. Each time, the fantasy ended with their lips pressed together, their bodies intertwined.

Mia did that sort of thing all the time. Hell, if Mia were in her shoes – and if Mia liked men – she would have probably had Carson Smith against the wall of the student center by now.

"Get a grip, Riley," she muttered to herself, forcing her attention back to the task at hand.

After an exhausting several hours of attempting to hold herself upright and expounding on one hundred level political science to disinterested freshmen, Riley wandered back to her office. As soon as she sat down at her desk, someone was immediately at the door.

"Dr. Whittaker?" a timid voice called out, breaking the silence. Riley looked up to see one of her students standing in the doorway, clutching an essay. – Jenny maybe? There were a bunch of Jennys this year.

"Come in, Jenny," Riley beckoned, disappointed she couldn't sneak in a nap and really hoping she got the name right. They discussed the student's paper, and Riley offered suggestions for improvement. When Jenny left, another student was at the door. And then another. Followed by another. There was no respite in sight.

As the day went on, her office hours were followed by another lecture, an hour listening to one of her colleagues complain about students on phones, and a meeting on department policy that dragged on so long that Riley wanted to drill a hole in her head.

So, an average Wednesday, really.

At the end of her day, she collapsed back into her office. "Only a few more emails," she told herself. "Then you can get out of here and shower."

As the clock struck six o'clock, Riley decided to give up and closed her computer. At least she'd gotten everything graded that she needed to, and she had no shot of being any more productive at this point. She gathered her belongings, tucking some spare papers and her laptop into her bag. The dimming light from the setting autumn sun cast shadows across the floor, sending a shiver down her spine as memories of the the night before resurfaced. She shook her head, more tired than scared.

"Focus on what you can do, not what you can't," she told herself.

As Riley stepped into the hallway, her eyes met Carson's smoldering gaze from across the corridor. His dark hair framed his face, highlighting his chiseled features and pervasive eyes that seemed to look straight into her soul.

"Riley," he said, his voice rich like molten chocolate. "Fancy meeting you here."

"Immediately outside my office doors at the end of my day? Who'dve thought," she replied, trying to keep her voice steady as her heart raced. "Just finishing up, how about you, Dr. Smith?"

"Just got out of the most boring meeting of my life," he said, taking a few steps closer. The distance between them shrank rapidly, their bodies practically magnetized. "Allow me to walk you to your car?"

"Sure," she agreed, feeling the warmth of his presence as they began walking side by side. "I know what those meetings are like."

As they strolled through the campus, the golden rays of the setting sun filtering through the trees cast a warm glow on their faces. Carson turned to Riley, his eyes dancing with mischief. "You know, I've heard rumors about you, Riley Whittaker."

"Really?" Riley raised an eyebrow, intrigued. "Do share."

"Word has it that you're as captivating outside the classroom as you are in it," he said, his voice low and seductive. "I must admit, I'm curious to find out for myself."

Riley felt a blush creep up her neck, but she met his gaze boldly. "Well, Carson Smith, I could say the same. Your reputation precedes you as well."

"Is that so?" Carson smirked, clearly enjoying their flirtatious banter.

"Absolutely," Riley replied, her voice sultry. "I've heard you can make even the driest historical events come alive with passion and intrigue."

"I certainly try to, though I'm never sure if I'm successful," he confessed, his eyes never leaving hers. "But enough about me. Tell me what brought you to Garrity University. You're about two decades younger than anyone else in your department."

Riley considered for a moment before answering, the anticipation in the air palpable. "Garrity's Political Science faculty is certainly 'mature,'" she said with a small laugh. "I guess I'd just have to admit I like the pace in a smaller college town. It holds its secrets well, just like I enjoy keeping mine."

"Ah, a kindred spirit," Carson smiled, his eyes gleaming with approval. "I find the city too distracting. Too noisy. I taught in New York before this, and it's just sometimes far too much… and of course, I have my own secrets too."

He was handsome, he was smart, and he had an edge of mystery that Riley found herself being drawn into. Yes he was probably fifteen years older than her, but if that was his biggest flaw, Riley thought she could do a lot worse.

After a few moments they reached her car, a deep green sedan that had seen better days, parked beneath an old oak tree.

"Thank you for the company, Carson," Riley said, her voice laced with genuine warmth.

"Of course," he replied, his gaze lingering on her eyes. "It's not every day I get to share time with such a captivating soul."

Riley felt her cheeks flush at the compliment, the heat spreading across her face like wildfire. She shifted her weight from one foot to the other, feeling the cool, damp earth compress beneath her shoes. *God, has it been* that *long since I flirted with someone? Get it together, Riley.*

"So this may sound strange, but you know the alumni fundraiser on Thursday?" Carson asked, his confident voice tinged with vulnerability. "All of the department heads are required to be there, and they're incredibly boring."

"I know about it, I wasn't planning on going?" Riley answered. "The advantage of being so low on the food chain is that no one actually cares if I go to those things."

"Yes, well… I don't get a choice, but I was hoping to choose my company," Carson said with a glint in his eye. "I was wondering if you would like to come with me as my plus one? We can continue our conversation about small towns and secrets."

Riley's heart raced, pounding in her ears like a bongo drum. Her fingers brushed against the cold metal of her car keys, suddenly feeling very conscious of every sensation – the texture of her slacks, the softness of her blouse against her skin, the faint taste of coffee on her tongue.

"I'd like that," she managed to say, meeting his intense gaze with a shy smile.

"Great," he grinned, taking a step back to give her space. "Let me give you my number and you can text me your address. I'll swing by your place at eight?"

"Sounds perfect," Riley agreed, her pulse still racing. Carson quickly jotted down his information, and slid it into Riley's hand, his touch lingering a fraction longer than he needed to.

As Carson turned to leave, Riley couldn't help but feel like they were being watched. She glanced around the dimming parking lot, her eyes searching for any sign of movement.

A shadow detached itself from the darkness near the edge of the lot, its form indistinct. For a moment, Riley's heart clenched with fear, her mind racing with possibilities – but then the figure vanished into the night, leaving nothing behind but the faint rustle of leaves.

Riley shook off the unsettling feeling, attributing it to her overactive imagination. Unlocking her car, she took one last look at Carson's retreating figure before getting in, her thoughts moving to their upcoming date and the secrets they might share together.

Chapter 5

Daniel sprinted through the dark park trail, his heart pounding in sync with each desperate footfall. The gnarled branches above him cast twisted shadows on the damp ground, making it difficult to see where he was going. His muscles burned from exertion, but terror pushed him forward, fueled by the knowledge that his pursuer was relentless.

The shadowy figure on his heals was cold and calculating. They seemed to be able to predict where Daniel was running before he did. Their deadly eyes were fixed firmly on his every move.

"Can't run forever, kid," a cold, feminine voice called out from the darkness.

"Leave me alone!" Daniel shouted back, his voice cracking under the strain of fear and physical exhaustion. He stumbled over an exposed root but managed to catch himself before falling, panic driving him to keep moving despite the ache in his legs.

The figure closed the distance between them with blinding speed, her body low to the ground and her movements fluid and predatory. This woman was a monster, and Daniel knew he had to get away.

"Got you!" the figure exclaimed as she lunged at Daniel, tackling him to the muddy ground with a bone-jarring impact. Her grip on his wrists was like steel, her fingers digging into his flesh as he struggled in vain beneath her. She was only a few inches shorter than he was, and looked like she was in her late twenties. Her short brown hair framed a face as cold as a winter's night, and wore a leather jacket and jeans.

If Daniel had seen her on the street, he would have said she was pretty – but her cold, dark eyes made her the most terrifying thing he had ever witnessed.

"Please, don't!" Daniel pleaded, his eyes wide with fear. But his cries for mercy only seemed to fuel the fire within her.

"Did you really think you could escape?" she taunted, her voice dripping with venomous satisfaction. "Nobody escapes."

"Please," Daniel gasped once more, his voice barely a whisper as he stared up at her with pleading eyes. "I don't want to die."

"Nobody does – it doesn't mean you get a choice," she said coldly. Something told Daniel that this woman didn't feel much of anything. "You certainly didn't give that girl a choice."

Just as she seemed primed to deliver a final blow, Daniel's face contorted in a way that seemed impossible. His jaw open wide and almost unhinged, revealing a pair of razor sharp fangs that glinted like daggers in the moonlight.

"Finally showing off. Is that supposed to scare me?" the woman hissed through gritted teeth.

"It should," he replied smugly, attempting to twist free from her grasp. He managed to push her off of him, and then lunged at her with his newfound strength, his fangs aiming for the tender flesh of her throat.

Their bodies collided, and a well placed elbow struck Daniel's sternum. The force of it sent him rolling across the damp ground. He was back on his feet in a moment, and the scent of mud and decay filled the air. He launched himself back at the woman, and the two exchanged a flurry of blows.

"You're filth. Disgusting leeches," the woman spat, narrowly avoiding Daniel's snapping jaws. "Feeding on the innocent – killing people like they're nothing."

"Survival of the fittest," he countered, a twisted grin spreading across his monstrous face. "And a guy's gotta eat."

"Killers like you don't deserve to walk this earth," she snarled, her eyes almost on fire. "And I'm going to stop you."

"Over my undead body," he growled, taking another swing at the woman. He leaped back, readying himself for another assault.

"That's the plan," she whispered, her eyes locked onto his with unflinching determination. Their dance of death continued, punctuated by guttural snarls and primal screams.

Finally, she managed to land a well placed kick to Daniel's chest, sending him sprawling to the ground again. Coldly, she pinned him beneath her, one hand gripping his throat. She pulled a long silver dagger from her boot.

"Any last words?" she asked icily.

"Sarah, wait!" a voice called out, its urgency cutting through the tense air. Mia stood at the edge of the clearing, her breath ragged from running and her eyes wide with fear. "Don't kill him!"

The woman froze, but didn't release her grip on the vampire. The shock on her face broke the image of the perfect hunter she'd worked so hard to project. "M…Mia?"

"Yeah Sarah, it's me…" Mia said, her voice shaking.

"What the hell are you doing here?" Sarah responded. Her voice was full of uncertainty and surprise, but her grip on Daniel's throat still tightened.

"I live here. Sarah, please," Mia pleaded, her voice laced with a desperation that threatened to shatter the resolve of even the most hardened warrior. "I need him alive. He might have information I can use."

Sarah hesitated, her cold exterior cracking as she weighed the consequences of her actions. The long blade in her hand trembled, unsure of what to do.

"Fine," Sarah spat through gritted teeth, releasing Daniel's throat and rising to her feet. The vampire gasped for air, his eyes full of fear and confusion.

"Stop being a baby, you don't even need to breathe," Sarah said, rolling her eyes.

"Thank you," Mia whispered, her relief palpable. She turned to face Daniel, her eyes boring into him. She might be worse than the first one. "You're going to tell us everything you know. Understand?"

Daniel nodded weakly, his fangs still bared but the fight gone from his eyes.

"Where are we taking him," Sarah said grudgingly, grabbing Daniel by the arm and pulling him to his feet.

"To Lucy's. She's a friend," Mia said, grabbing Daniel by the other arm. "And before you freak out, yes she's a vampire... but, like, a good vampire?"

"A 'good' vampire?" Sarah paused for a moment. "What do you mean a 'good' vampire?"

"Like one who doesn't hurt people," Mia said, walking forward and crossing the distance. "She's just–"

"God, you've slept with this woman, haven't you," Sarah said, rolling her eyes.

"That is... that's not..." Mia stammered. "Jesus, we don't speak for almost two years and you're asking if I've fucked the first woman who's come up in conversation?"

"You *have* slept with her though," Sarah said. "But fine, we'll see your 'good' vampire."

"Don't attack or kill her," Mia said quietly.

"Fine."

"I mean it."

"I know. I won't attack her or kill her, I promise," Sarah said in a tone so cold and flat Mia couldn't quite parse the intention.

As they began their trek through the dark park trail, Mia couldn't help but cast a sidelong glance at Sarah. Her mind was a whirlwind of emotions, each threatening to consume her. This was surreal, and there was so much she wanted to say – but dealing with their captive had to take priority.

"Are you sure this is the right decision?" Sarah asked, her voice barely audible above the sound of rustling leaves underfoot. "We could just kill him and go talk about why I'm here."

Mia's eyes never left the path ahead, but her voice held a note of conviction that seemed to defy her own doubts. "We need answers, and he's our best lead. We'll deal with whatever comes next when we don't have an undead audience."

"Fine," Sarah muttered again, her grip on Daniel's arm tightening. "Let's just get this over with."

Mia shook her head. Sarah wasn't the same person Mia used to know. How could she be? She'd lost a part of herself saving Mia that could never come back. Mia's soul was intact because Sarah sacrificed half of her own. It was absolutely insane that she was here in Parrish Mills, let alone had been tracking the same vampire that she had.

But god, it was so good to see her again.

Chapter 6

Mia stepped out of Sarah's car into the cold night air. Lucy's house loomed before her, its dark windows and silvered edges casting an eerie glow in the moonlight. Sarah emerged from the driver's seat, her breath fogging in the chill as she glanced up at the imposing structure.

"Lucy's place?" she asked, a hint of skepticism lacing her tone. "Because it seems like half of this town is spooky Victorian houses, and this entire neighborhood looks like it's owned by vampires."

"Yeah, this is it," Mia confirmed, leading the way to the door. Sarah dragged Daniel out of the back seat, and pulled him along by the scruff of his neck. In many ways the captured vampire resembled an angry, wet cat. The trio ascended the porch steps, the wood creaking beneath their weight.

Lucy opened the door before they could knock, her eyes scanning their faces, lingering on Daniel. "Bring him inside," she commanded, her voice cold and precise.

As Mia and Sarah guided Daniel through the threshold, Lucy's gaze met Mia's, and she raised a questioning eyebrow. Mia tilted her head silently and gave a small shrug.

With a graceful sweep of her arm, Lucy gestured for them to follow her towards the basement door.

Descending the dimly lit staircase, the musty scent of old wood and damp earth filled their nostrils. The basement was spacious, with stone walls and a dirt floor. At the far end, Emma paced restlessly, her fangs bared in anticipation.

"Keep an eye on him," Lucy instructed Emma, nodding to the captive vampire. Emma shot a dangerous grin toward Daniel, her eyes gleaming with malice. As Lucy locked the basement door behind them, Mia felt a shiver run down her spine – it was impossible to tell which vampire was more dangerous.

"You could have given me some warning that you'd be bringing a prisoner here," Lucy sighed, walking Mia and Sarah to the living room.

"This wasn't planned," Mia replied. "And again, *you don't have a phone*."

As they reached the living room, the front door swung open, revealing a flushed Riley. Her eyes sparkled with excitement, and she practically danced into the room.

"Hey, Mia!" she exclaimed, her voice slightly breathless. "You won't believe what hap–"

Her words died in her throat as she caught sight of Sarah, her expression shifting from giddy to startled. Mia braced herself for the questions she knew would follow.

"Whomst the fuck?" Riley stammered, her eyes darting between the two women.

"You must be Riley. Mia told me about you on the drive over," Sarah greeted her flatly, crossing her arms over her chest, her posture defensive.

"Riley, this is Sarah," Mia said quickly. She could feel the tension radiating off of her ex-girlfriend, and had to try very hard not to roll her eyes.

"Uh, hey," Riley managed before turning to Mia, her eyes narrowing with suspicion. "And you know her how?"

"Why is your name so god damned common..." Mia murmured, rubbing her temples as she tried to make sense of the whirlwind evening. She wished she could share her thoughts with Riley because trying to put these feelings into words was damned near impossible. "It's *Sarah* Sarah. Sarah Masters."

Riley blinked for a moment like her brain was rebooting. "As in the ex you spent over a decade extreme trauma bonding with? The one who lost half her soul saving you Sarah?"

"Apparently," Sarah said flatly.

"This sounds like the three of you need to talk. Maybe we should all sit down and do that," Lucy suggested, her eyes flicking between the three women. She gestured to the plush couches and chairs that filled the warmly lit living room.

As they settled into their seats, Mia couldn't help but notice the way Sarah's gaze lingered on her. Mia wasn't sure if that was a good thing or a bad thing. She swallowed hard, willing her racing heart to calm itself. Memories beckoned that she didn't have time to revisit. The night was far from over, and she needed to keep her emotions in check – for everyone's sake.

"But seriously, *Sarah*," Riley shook her head. "The same Sarah you cried so much over. That Sarah."

"You... cried?" Sarah said, slowly.

"What brings you to Parrish Mills, then?" Riley interrupted quickly.

"Yes, sorry," Sarah responded in a controlled tone. She was almost unnervingly still as she sat, but her voice held a hint of bitterness that Mia couldn't quite place. "I'm here because I've been tracking a vampire – one who goes by the name of the Drake."

"The Drake?" Lucy questioned, leaning forward with interest. "I've heard whispers about him over the centuries. You're sure he's here?"

"Yes," Sarah nodded, her jaw set with determination. "No one seems to know much about him, but I'm convinced he's planning something – and he's planning it *here*."

Lucy shook her head. "That is concerning news. Anything someone like that could be planning would likely put everyone in danger – humans and vampires alike."

"Someone like that in town, and two recently turned vampires running around?" Mia murmured, her thoughts racing as she tried to wrap her head around the information. "That's definitely not coincidence."

"Understatement of the year," Sarah agreed coldly. "I've been hunting him for the last six months, and I followed the Drake's trail here."

Moonlight filtered through the gauzy curtains, casting an ethereal glow upon the faces of the four women as the seriousness of the situation set in. The air carried a palpable tension that seemed to cling to Mia's skin like a second layer.

"Allow me to help you in your hunt, Sarah," Lucy said, her voice low and smooth – a sensuous purr that entwined itself around the words. "If the Drake is in Parrish Mills, then it is my responsibility to put an end to his machinations and protect those I care for."

Sarah hesitated for a moment, her eyes flicking between Mia and Lucy, as if coldly weighing the pros and cons of accepting the vampire's help. Finally, she nodded, though her face was full of tension. "Thank you, Lucy. Your knowledge of the vampire world will be… invaluable."

Mia shifted uncomfortably as she watched a wolf and a tiger agree to make nice.

"Where are you staying in Parrish Mills?" Lucy asked Sarah, concern etched into the fine lines of her ageless face.

"Uh, just my car," Sarah admitted, with a shrug. "I didn't have time to make any arrangements."

"Please, consider my home your base of operations while you're here," Lucy offered, gesturing towards the opulent surroundings. "I have plenty of empty rooms, and it's safe and secure. I can provide some useful resources for your investigation possibly too. Just stay out of the basement and the attic unless I'm with you."

"Thank you, Lucy," Sarah replied, in a flat tone. "I appreciate your generosity." Her supposed gratitude wasn't all that convincing, but she also seemed like she wasn't going to fight it. "If it's not rude to ask, may I ask why those areas are off limits?"

"Vampire that still needs to be housebroken in the basement and likely-agoraphobic human girlfriend in the attic," Riley responded quickly. "Emma's mean, Jayla's nice, and yes it's all pretty fucked up if you think about it too hard."

"Let me show you where you can put your things," Lucy said, standing up and ignoring Riley.

Lucy led Sarah and Mia up the stairs and down a dimly lit hallway towards one of the large house's spare bedrooms. Shadows danced across the opulent wallpaper, reflecting the tension that hung in the air like a thick fog. The scent of burning wax mixed with age-old wood, creating a unique aroma that was both comforting and strange.

"Here we are," Lucy announced, opening the door to reveal a lavish room adorned with antique furniture and luxurious fabrics. "I hope this will be suitable for your stay, Sarah."

"More than suitable, thank you," Sarah replied, her voice almost clinically detached.

"Please make yourself at home," Lucy said, her eyes meeting Mia's for a brief moment before she turned on her heel and left the two women alone.

As the door clicked shut behind Lucy, the weight of their shared history seemed to descend like a bag of bricks on Mia and Sarah, filling the room with a palpable weight. Sarah's gaze was cold, distant, a far cry from the warmth that she used to look at Mia with.

"Nice friends you've found yourself here," Sarah remarked, her tone laced with sarcasm as she peered around the room.

"Lucy and I aren't close, she just doesn't want to see anyone hurt," Mia replied, feeling defensive. "I'm just trying to help keep people safe here."

"Of course," Sarah said, her eyes narrowing. "Always the helper."

Mia clenched her jaw, the sting of Sarah's words cutting through her defenses. "Look, I didn't ask you to come here, Sarah."

"Right, because I actually pay attention to what's happening in the world," Sarah shot back, anger simmering beneath the surface of her words. "Unlike you, who seems content to just hide away in some random small town, pretending your past doesn't exist. Pretending that I don't exist."

"Stop it, Sarah," Mia warned, her voice shaking with unspoken emotion. "You don't know what I've been through."

"I *do* know Mia, I was there, remember?" Sarah whispered, her voice cracking as she closed the distance between them. "I'm the one who paid the price for what we did. I didn't get to run away from the repercussions."

The two stood there, and Mia shifted uncomfortably, her eyes cast towards the floor.

"I still dream about you," Mia said quietly. "Sometimes they're just memories, sometimes they're more. I keep trying to find ways to say I'm sorry for what I did to you."

"What is it that you think you did," Sarah replied. "Because I think you might be apologizing for the wrong thing and not what actually hurt me."

The room sat silently for a moment, Mia felt like she was standing in quicksand.

"So when did you start hunting," Mia asked quietly.

"Not long after you left," Sarah responded, shifting uncomfortably. "I was crawling out of my skin and needed to do something."

"You always were good at protecting people," Mia said quietly. "It suits you."

"You really went through with the whole 'magic tattoo plan.' I never thought you'd actually do it. One was already kind of ridiculous," Sarah said, a hint of a smile almost reaching her lips.

"Why do I feel like you've said that to me before?" Mia whispered.

"I don't know, but it doesn't really feel like two years have passed sometimes," Sarah said, moving towards Mia. "I think a part of me is bound to you still."

"I think a part of us is still in that warehouse," Mia sighed.

"Sometimes I think that too," Sarah replied, her stone face softening.

"I've missed you. I've thought about reaching out a million times, but I didn't think you'd want to hear from me," Mia said, brushing a curl of black hair out of her eyes.

"I've missed you too," Sarah said in a voice barely above a whisper. "I don't know if I've really felt like myself without you nearby."

Their eyes locked, a storm of unspoken words and emotions swirling between them. And then, without warning, their lips met – a desperate, passionate clash that seemed to momentarily eclipse the pain of their past.

As they pulled apart, their breaths mingling in the charged air, Mia realized that despite everything, the connection between them still remained – a twisted, tangled web of love and betrayal that refused to be severed.

"This is probably a bad idea," Mia said, catching her breath.

"I don't think I really care right now." Sarah grabbed Mia, and kissed her again.

As the intensity of their kiss grew, Mia felt herself being pulled into a vortex of desire and need. The taste of Sarah's lips, the scent of her skin – it was all intoxicating, impossible to resist. Their bodies moved in sync, as if remembering an ancient dance only they knew.

"Sarah..." Mia breathed, her fingers digging into the other woman's shoulders, their eyes locked together. "I think..."

"Stop talking," Sarah whispered urgently, cutting off Mia's protests with another searing kiss. Her hands roamed over Mia's body, tracing the curves and contours with a desperate familiarity. It was as if she were trying to commit every inch of Mia to memory, even as they both knew this encounter was likely just borrowed time.

Mia surrendered to the passion that ignited in her veins, the ghosts of their shared history swept away on a tide of sensations. Their clothes were quickly tossed aside, leaving a trail of fabric and leather that led to the bed where they tangled together, limbs entwined. Each touch, each caress, became a declaration of love and need. Their bodies hungered for each other after a long fast.

As Sarah's lips found the sensitive spot on Mia's neck, the witch let out a soft moan, her hands clutching the sheets. Every nerve ending seemed to come alive under Sarah's skilled hands, a familiar, primal need sweeping through Mia like an unparalleled force.

"God, I missed you," Mia gasped between kisses, her legs wrapping around Sarah's waist as they moved together. "I never wanted to leave..."

"Then don't leave again," Sarah begged, her voice raw with emotion as their bodies collided again and again. "Stay with me, Mia. We can face whatever comes together."

But even as the pleasure threatened to overwhelm her, Mia couldn't ignore the nagging voice in the back of her mind – the one that reminded her of the demons they'd both faced, and the price they'd paid for their addiction.

"Don't ask me to make promises I don't know if I can keep," Mia whispered as she finally succumbed to passion, their bodies trembling in the aftermath.

****

Morning light poured through the coffee shop window as Mia nursed her latte waiting for Riley to arrive. The events of the previous night still lingered in her mind, the taste of Sarah's lips and the feel of her body imprinted on her memory like a brand. It was a ridiculously stupid thing to have done, but Mia couldn't deny how much she missed her.

"Hey," Riley said as she slid into the booth across from Mia, her eyes searching her friend's face with concern.

"You doing okay there sport? I had to leave last night while you were… busy."

"Sorry about that," Mia replied, struggling to find the words to explain what had happened between her and Sarah. "Riley... I never told you what happened with me and Sarah. Not fully."

"Okay, I'm here to listen," Riley replied. "Whatever it is, I've got you."

"This is... this is going to sound fucked up and weird," Mia sighed.

"We've been hanging out with a vampire who has her girlfriend in an attic," Riley said shaking her head. "How fucked up and weird can it be comparatively?"

"You say that but... you know that Sarah and I, we were addicted to something dangerous. We used to summon demons, letting them possess us," Mia said quietly. "We did it for the high. It was incredibly dangerous and damaging to both of us."

"I know, Mia," Riley replied, a concerned look on her face. "You've told me this before. Like in the first week that we met. It comes up a lot, frankly. Like *this week* a lot. You got possessed to get high, yadda yadda yadda, and it all ended after she burned away half of her soul to save you."

"That is the *beginning* of the story, Riley," Mia admitted, taking a shaky sip of her coffee. "What I did after... wasn't great. There's not exactly a map for 'recovering from demonic possession addiction,' but I'm pretty sure I fucked it all up."

Riley reached across the table, her hand covering Mia's in a gesture of support. "Whatever you need, I'm here for you. What happened?"

"The first few days, we both decided we'd never use again. Sarah wanted me to swear off magic altogether, but I just couldn't do it," Mia shifted nervously in her seat. "She didn't talk to me for weeks, and I just couldn't handle it. I needed magic to protect myself from my own addiction, to remove my temptation, and she just wanted me to need her."

Riley nodded, listening carefully.

"So I left… I stayed in Boston for a while, and started getting my tattoos. I burned through almost all of my money, and did some things I'm not proud of to finance my survival," Mia sighed. "All the while, I made sure Sarah didn't see me or know where I was. After almost a year, I realized that even being that close to my old life was too much of a temptation, so I picked a random place on a map, found the cheapest apartment I could, and relocated here… never telling Sarah where I went."

"So she didn't know you were here?" Riley asked, surprised. "I was assuming you were a part of why she came."

"I don't know, maybe I was," Mia whispered. Mia stared into the milky brown swirls of her coffee, the steam wafting up and brushing against her cheeks. The bitter aroma enveloped her senses as she lost herself in memories. She clenched her hands around the cup, the heat seeping through the ceramic and warming her fingers. "I think she and I are bound together sometimes. It's hard to deny it when she's still in the room."

"I assume that tension is why she was so distant when I first got to the house?" Riley asked carefully, trying to piece together the complex relationship between Mia and Sarah.

"Partly," Mia admitted, her gaze drifting back to the window where sunlight danced on the pavement. "But also she's *always* been a bit like that. Sarah doesn't like new people. I'm just not used to it being directed towards me too."

"This is a lot, Mia," Riley said shaking her head. "But if there's anything you need me to do, tell me. Even if I don't know what the right thing is, I want you to know I'll do it if you ask."

"Thanks Riley," Mia said sighing. "I don't know what I'd do without you."

"Be really sad and lonely and have no one to tell stories about who you've hooked up with?" Riley said with a wink.

"Probably," Mia sighed. "Also… I slept with Sarah last night…"

"Oh, I know. We *all* know. The walls in Lucy's house are *not* thick, and I was in the living room," Riley said with a laugh. "Hell, Lucy says Emma could hear it in the *basement*."

"Well... fuck," Mia said, relaxing a bit.

"Are you two getting back together?" Riley asked carefully.

"I don't think so?" Mia said, her voice raising an octave by the end of the sentence. "We didn't really talk that much? I *did* tell her about Bobbi?"

"Yeah, I expect that'll be fun to unpack," Riley smiled while shaking her head. "Especially whenever you get around to interrogating the fanged frat boy."

"We're doing that today," Mia said, laying her head on the table. "We're just waiting until I'm done with work."

"Honestly ask Jayla to record that, because I kind of want to watch the legendarily smooth Mia Graves be a train wreck," Riley snickered.

"You're being really supportive right now," Mia said, still head down on the coffee shop table.

"I know, right? Now enough about you and vampires and demons – let me tell you about how the hot head of the history department asked me out," Riley smiled. "He's taking me to this faculty event tonight, and his ass is amazing."

Chapter 7

The creak of the basement door seeped into the dimly lit room, announcing Mia and Sarah's entrance. A single bulb cast shadows on the walls, accentuating the tension hanging in the air. As the door clicked shut behind them, Sarah's eyes scanned the space with clinical precision, her demeanor icy and detached.

"Remember, stay focused. If we want information, you can't get waylaid," Sarah instructed, her voice devoid of emotion.

Mia nodded silently, feeling oddly calm as she took in the sight before her: the vampire, Daniel, restrained to a chair in the center of the room. At first glance, he appeared to be just another ordinary college student, with his tousled brown hair and dark-rimmed glasses. But as they approached, his face contorted into a snarl, exposing the elongated fangs that betrayed his true nature.

"Oh, super scary," Mia taunted, her voice dripping with sarcasm. "You'll have to do better than that."

"Please take this seriously, Mia," Sarah warned, her expression unchanging as she observed the scene from a calculated distance.

"I am taking this seriously," Mia muttered, ignoring Sarah's caution and stepping closer to the creature. "It's not like he can bite me."

"He can't bite *you*," Sarah replied.

Daniel sneered at their approach in a futile attempt to intimidate them. But beneath his bravado, Mia could see the fear lurking in his eyes – a primal terror that betrayed a surface of defiance. She knew, deep down, that the monster before her was as desperate as he was dangerous.

"Are you ready to talk?" Mia asked, her voice steady. Lots of things stressed Mia out, but this was her element. This was where she was at home.

"Go to hell," Daniel spat in resistance, even as his eyes darted around the room. He was clearly searching for any means of escape.

"Been there, done that," Mia replied coolly. Frankly she had invited in far scarier things into her life than a single vampire tied to a chair. "Now, let's try that again, shall we?"

As Mia pressed Daniel for information, she couldn't help but notice Sarah's unwavering focus, the way her cold gaze never left the vampire's face. Mia was tempted to wondered if what Sarah had lost had made her colder, but in many ways Sarah had *always* been like this.

How much of a person *was* their soul anyway?

"Tell us what you know," Mia demanded, her voice carrying a note of urgency as she pushed aside her memories and focused on the task at hand. "What do you know about the Drake?"

"He's your worst nightmare," Daniel replied, his tone smug despite his obvious fear. "You have no idea what's coming."

"Enlighten us," Mia shot back, her patience wearing thin. "Or I'll make sure you never see another sunset."

"Empty threats won't break me," Daniel snarled, his eyes narrowing as he tried to gauge her sincerity. "But if it's a fight you want, you'll get one."

"Fine, we can do this the fun way," Mia smirked as she clenched her fists. "But don't say I didn't warn you."

"Enough," Sarah interjected, her icy demeanor finally cracking as she stepped forward. "We're not here to play games. We need answers, and we need them now."

"Then ask a different question," Daniel hissed, his fangs gleaming menacingly in the dim light.

Mia grabbed a metal chair from the corner and pulled it across the room with a screech as the legs dragged across the rough basement floor. She sat down across from the captured vampire, and her dark eyes, unwavering and resolute, locked onto his. Sarah stood behind her with a posture rigid like bear trap, ready to snap.

"Are you really so confident?" Mia asked, her voice steady but filled with curiosity. "You're tied up, powerless, and at our mercy."

Daniel smiled. His sunken cheeks seemed to hollow out even further as he spoke, giving him an eerie, skeletal appearance. "I may be bound, sweetheart, but I'm far from powerless," he taunted, the words dripping with venom.

The air thickened around them as if charged with electricity, and Mia felt the hairs on her arms rise. He was going to try something, Mia was certain, but she wasn't sure *what*.

"The smug asshole thing isn't really going to get you anywhere, were you this annoying before you got turned?" Mia retorted, trying to keep herself from smirking too much. "You really strike me as the kind of guy who was already like this."

"You won't get me to talk and neither will your psycho girlfriend, witch," Daniel sneered, his gaze directed at the leather clad Sarah. "But don't worry. You'll learn soon enough what real power is – and just how insignificant you truly are."

"God, you *are* just an ordinary college fuckboy with delusions of grandeur," Mia sighed. "Like you're not even *scary*. Don't get me wrong, there are scary ass vampires in the world, but you are *definitely* not one of them."

"Is that so?" he retorted, his pale blue eyes boring into hers. "Perhaps I'll just have to prove you wrong."

As the verbal sparring continued, Mia's mind raced. She knew that if they were to stand any chance of stopping the Drake, they needed information, and they needed it from this jackass. But what if he didn't actually know anything? What if this guy really was just an idiot?

Ignoring Daniel's taunts, Mia looked him straight in the eye and asked, "What is the Drake doing? Why is he turning people?"

"Ah," Daniel smirked. "You want to know about our numbers? Our base of operations? You think I'd just give you information about the Drake's grand army?"

"Indulge me," Mia replied coolly, her fingertips drumming against the armrest of her chair in a rhythmic cadence. "Or are you too afraid of your own kind knowing what you've told us?"

Daniel let out a low chuckle, shaking his head in mock disbelief. "Very well," he drawled, his voice dripping with condescension. "I'll tell you what you want to know. But it won't matter. You can't stop us. He has dozens – no, hundreds – of loyal followers, all under his command."

"Where is he?" Mia demanded. Maybe he didn't know anything. Maybe he was lying. But if they could just get a single piece of workable intelligence on the Drake's identity, it would help. This whole "army" thing was definitely disconcerting.

"People like you are always so eager for answers," Daniel mused, his eyes narrowing into dangerous slits. "The Drake moves through your mortal world like it was nothing. He walks among the weak, hidden in plain sight. He gathers us here, turning us... testing us... making sure only the strongest of his offspring survive. Soon, there won't be a single soul left untainted by our touch."

"Is that all?" Mia scoffed. "Just another band of bloodthirsty monsters, claiming to be unstoppable?"

"Far from it," Daniel hissed, leaning forward, the veins in his neck standing out starkly against his pale skin. "We are more than mere vampires. We are the heralds of a new age, the vanguard of the night that will sweep across this world and reshape it in our image. There is a great darkness coming, and when it arrives the Drake will stand beside it and usurp it. We will march forward into the new order as its leaders. He has foreseen it all, and there is nothing you or anyone else can do to stop it."

Mia sat with this for a moment, sorting through the layers of arrogance and conviction in the vampire's words. Was he lying? Exaggerating? Clearly this guy was drinking the Kool Aid.

"Bit overconfident there, bud," Mia warned, her voice almost a sigh.

"Perhaps," Daniel replied, his eyes locked on hers. "But I assure you, we will have the last laugh."

Mia glanced at Sarah, the standing woman's eyes wide and fierce as they met hers. Sarah's face was the image of determination, but it wasn't clear how much of this was a mask.

"Tell us where to find the Drake," Mia demanded, her voice ice-cold as she tried to maintain control over the interrogation.

"Maybe I should start cutting bits off of him, to encourage an answer," Sarah said quietly. Mia glared at her silently.

"Even if I knew, I wouldn't tell you," Daniel spat, his voice dripping with disdain. He shifted uncomfortably in his bindings, his agitation growing more apparent with each passing moment. His calm demeanor was starting to crumble.

Mia clenched her fists, her nails digging into her palms. She felt a surge of dark energy pulse through her tattoos. It was tempting to use some sort of magic on the vampire to find out what he knew, but those spells always risked only showing you what you *wanted* to see instead of the truth — especially when cast on an unwilling participant.

"Your loser-ass leader is going to fail, I mean he's starting in Parrish Mills of all places," Mia smirked. "Not exactly the epicenter of world power."

"Your words prove you know nothing of what's to come, of the world we will usher in," Daniel sneered. His eyes darted around the room, searching for an escape route, as the interrogation intensified. Sweat beaded on his forehead, his breathing becoming more labored.

"He knows he doesn't have to breathe, right?" Sarah muttered. "Why does this idiot keep doing that."

"Tell me, vampire, do you truly believe that your kind can rule this world?" Mia asked, her tone mocking. "A lot of you can't even be outside in the sunlight."

"Of course," he replied, defiance evident in every word. "The Drake has shown us the way. We are destined to rise above the petty constraints of this world and ascend to our rightful place as its rulers."

"Destined. Sure. We totally believe you," Mia said wryly, her gaze never leaving his face.

"Enough!" Daniel roared, his fangs bared as he strained against his bonds, muscles rippling beneath his skin. His eyes continued to dart around the room, panic seeping into his expression.

Sarah stepped closer, her posture tense and ready for action. Mia could feel the heat of Sarah's anger like a living thing, radiating outwards as if daring Daniel to make another move.

In a sudden burst of strength, Daniel's restraints snapped like brittle twigs. His eyes, once filled with fear, now burned with an almost feral determination. Before Mia or Sarah could react, he lunged towards the door, breaking through it and heading towards the basement stairs.

"Damn it!" Mia cursed under her breath, adrenaline surging through her veins as she sprinted after the fleeing vampire. Sarah was right on her heels, their footsteps echoing in unison as they chased Daniel up the stairs.

"Get back here, you moron! It's three in the afternoon! There's nowhere to run to!" Sarah shouted, her anger palpable as she raced to catch up with him.

Mia knew that if Daniel managed to escape, there was a good chance he'd burn up immediately. He was a new vampire, and definitely didn't have enough control over his powers to resist daylight. They wouldn't be able to follow up on anything he'd given them, and they'd have one less route for information.

"Almost there… almost there..." Mia thought, her lungs burning as she pursued the vampire.

With a final burst of speed, Daniel threw open the back door and stumbled out into the bright afternoon sun. The instant the sunlight touched his skin, it began to sizzle and smoke.

"Ah!" Daniel screamed, his voice a mix of fear and agony. As his body writhed in pain, the smell of seared flesh filled the air. Despite his suffering, the corners of his mouth twisted upward into a deranged smile. "You think this will stop us? You think you've won? The Drake's power is greater than you can possibly imagine!"

"Shut up, you delusional freak and get back inside!" Mia yelled as she finally reached the doorstep, watching the vampire's skin crack and blister in the unforgiving sunlight.

Sarah stood beside her, breathing heavily, her jaw clenched in frustration. "God damn it, what do we do now," she muttered, her eyes locked on the flaming figure before them.

"Get that blanket!" Mia yelled, pointing to a thick quilt lying discarded on the patio furniture. Sarah grabbed it, and together they sprinted towards the burning vampire.

"Daniel!" Mia shouted, her voice hoarse with desperation. She could feel the heat radiating off his body, making her sweat and her eyes sting. "Hold on!"

"Too late for me, you'll never stop him," he choked out through his twisted grin, even as his body continued to convulse in agony. The flames licked at his skin, forming grotesque patterns of charred flesh and seared muscle.

Mia and Sarah threw the blanket over him, but it was like trying to smother a raging inferno with a single sheet of paper. The fire devoured the fabric, leaving behind only ashes and the stench of burnt wool.

"Damn it!" Mia cursed, tears of frustration streaming down her cheeks. "That kid was probably only like twenty."

"He was a vampire who hurt people, he deserved it," Sarah replied grimly, her eyes blazing with determination. "I won't mourn one of those."

"No, the people the Drake is turning are victims too. This kid bought into it, but he didn't even remotely know the dangers," Mia said, staring at the pile of ashes that were all that was left of the vampire. Her thoughts turned to the countless lives at stake, and she felt the weight of their responsibility settle heavily on her shoulders. "This is entirely fucked. We need to piece together everything he said. If even half of it is true, we're in more danger than we thought."

"Agreed." Sarah's eyes remained locked on the smoldering remains. She really was just all walls right now. Mia wondered if anything could still touch her. "Let's start with what we know about the Drake."

"The moron claimed the Drake walked among us," Mia recalled, her fingers tracing the lines of one of her tattoos. "Which means he's likely completely immune to sunlight like Lucy is. Vampires like that are usually pretty old, and even then they're rare."

"Exactly," Sarah agreed. "Though a lot of normal vampires can spend a good hour outside before they go all... crispy critter." Sarah motioned towards the pile of ash on the ground that had once been Daniel.

"That's not a ton to go on," Mia declared, meeting Sarah's gaze with determination. "But he also acted like he knew about other vampires. For this idiot to even *know* about their existence means they must be meeting somewhere."

"True," Sarah replied, her jaw set in a fierce scowl. "So somewhere in this town there has to be a location they're using. A real world meeting place is a weakness we can find."

"Right," Mia agreed. "But we probably need to find another vampire to figure out where the hell that is."

Chapter 8

Riley Whittaker stood in front of her full-length mirror, scrutinizing her reflection as she adjusted the straps on her sleek black dress. The fabric clung to her curves, revealing enough to be enticing but still retaining an air of sophistication. She leaned in closer, applying a final coat of lipstick, and smiled at her reflection.

If only she felt as confident as she looked.

As she walked towards the door, Riley couldn't help but feel a pang of anxiety in her chest. It had been over a year since her ex-fiancé Jake had ended their engagement without warning. She'd had a few false starts, but this time she was determined to make it happen – even if putting herself out there was more terrifying than any monster that went bump in the night.

"Get a grip, Riley," she whispered to herself, taking a deep breath to steady her nerves. "It's just one night, and who knows? Maybe something wonderful will come out of it."

Or maybe you'll discover that he's got bodies buried in his basement, her inner voice chimed in. *With my record, that feels more in line.*

Riley crossed her fingers as she descended the stairs of the large, empty house. She paused in the foyer and looked back into the darkened halls. "Wish me luck everyone!" she called out into the echoing house. A ghostly chorus of whispers swirled through the empty rooms, and a gentle breeze seemed to push Riley towards the door.

With the encouragement of the spectral inhabitants of the Rose House, she stepped out onto the porch and into the cool autumn air.

Within moments, the purr of an engine drew Riley's gaze to the street as a black crossover pulled up in front of her house. Carson Smith, looking dashing in a tailored suit, emerged from the driver's seat with a confident stride that made her heart rate spike.

"Evening, Riley," he called out, his voice smooth and inviting. "You look stunning."

"Thank you," she replied, trying to sound casual but feeling her cheeks warm with a blush. "You clean up pretty well yourself."

Carson smirked, holding open the passenger door for her. As she slid into the plush leather seat, she couldn't help but appreciate the warmth radiating from him – a stark contrast to the chilly autumn air outside.

"Ready for a night of schmoozing and charming wealthy alumni out of their money?" he asked, starting the engine once more.

"Absolutely," Riley quipped, rolling her eyes playfully. "Nothing says 'thrilling evening' quite like pandering to people with deep pockets."

"Ah, the joys of academia," Carson sighed, merging onto the main road. "But hey, at least the drinks are free and we get to do it together."

"I must like you a lot," Riley smiled, stealing a glance at him. "Since I usually do my best to be invisible enough to avoid these things."

"I certainly hope so." Carson grinned, reaching across the center console to briefly squeeze her hand. "I promise, I'll be by your side all night, navigating the treacherous waters of university politics."

"Such a gallant knight to promise to protect me from the pit of vipers he's invited me into," Riley teased, a genuine smile tugging at her lips. "I'd better not catch you abandoning me for a glass of expensive scotch."

"Perish the thought!" he feigned shock. "Though, if you're partial to whiskey, I might be tempted to sneak away with you for a private toast."

"Deal," she agreed, feeling a flutter in her stomach at the thought of sharing a secret moment with him.

As the car sped along, Riley's mind raced with thoughts of what the night might hold. Would they share a dance? A stolen kiss in the moonlight? Or would it be nothing more than a mundane gathering filled with endless small talk.

"Hey," Carson said softly, sensing her unease. "Whatever happens tonight, just know that I'm glad you came."

"Hopefully I feel that way too," Riley murmured, taking comfort in his steady presence. She turned to face him, offering a genuine smile. "Now let's go conquer this fundraiser."

"Agreed," he replied, his eyes twinkling with determination as they continued their journey toward the unknown.

After a winding drive across town, the black crossover pulled up to the University President's stately home, its sprawling lawn dotted with meticulously trimmed hedges that seemed to whisper of wealth and power. Riley stared out the window, the opulence on display was, frankly, ridiculous considering how little she got paid.

"Ready for this?" Carson asked, his voice a soothing balm against her anxiety.

"About as ready as I'll ever be," she replied with a shaky laugh.

"I promise this will be fun," he said, winking at her as they stepped out of the car.

Riley nodded, taking a deep breath of the crisp autumn air. She clung to Carson's arm as they approached the entrance, where clusters of impeccably dressed alumni chatted animatedly beneath a grand archway, their laughter tinting the air with an air of insincerity.

"First rule of navigating these things," Carson whispered into her ear, "compliment everyone you meet. Flattery goes a long way."

"Got it," she murmured, steeling herself for the onslaught of schmoozing.

As they entered the opulent foyer, a woman in a vibrant red gown sashayed toward them, her smile as sharp as a knife. "Carson! You made it!" she exclaimed, wrapping him in a tight embrace that seemed more calculated than genuine.

"Of course, Marie," he replied smoothly, extricating himself from her grasp. "I wouldn't miss it for the world. And have I mentioned how stunning you look tonight?"

"Aw, you always know just what to say," she purred, her eyes flicking over to Riley. "And who is this lovely creature you've brought with you?"

"Riley Whittaker, Associate Professor of Political Science," he introduced her with pride. "Riley, meet Marie Jameson, one of our most esteemed alumni and CEO of AdderWave Technologies. She's the one who recommended me to the search committee."

"Charmed," Riley said, forcing a smile. "Your dress is absolutely breathtaking, Marie."

"Thank you, darling," Marie preened, clearly pleased with the compliment. "Well, I'll let you two mingle. Have fun!" With that, she glided away, leaving them to navigate the sea of expectant faces.

"See?" Carson grinned, giving her a reassuring squeeze. "You're a natural."

"Thanks, but let's not get ahead of ourselves," Riley muttered, trying to ignore the way her heart hammered in her chest. She turned to face him, seeking solace in his warm gaze. "Tell me where we're going, fearless captain."

"Right this way," he chuckled, guiding her through the throng of potential donors. As they made their way through the crowd, Riley found herself feeling more at ease with each interaction, her anxiety slowly dissolving under Carson's calming influence.

"Hey," he murmured, brushing a stray strand of hair from her face as they stood beneath a glittering chandelier. "You're doing great."

"Thanks," she replied, her cheeks flushing at his touch. "The secret is I'm treating them like they're five."

****

The hum of conversation and laughter from inside the opulent house faded as Riley stepped out onto the back terrace, seeking a moment of respite from the exhausting social dance she'd been immersed in for the last hour. The crisp autumn air was a welcome relief, her breath forming delicate clouds in front of her. She wrapped her arms around herself, feeling the soft fabric of her black dress against her skin.

"Nice view, isn't it?" Carson's voice drifted over to her, his presence both comforting and electrifying. He stood beside her, leaning against the ornate railing, his gaze fixed on the glittering stars above them. "I always find the night sky to be so... humbling."

Riley couldn't help but agree, staring up at the vast expanse of darkness, punctuated by pinpricks of light that had traveled millions of miles just to reach her eyes. With a deep breath, she tried to ignore her racing heart. "It really puts things into perspective," she murmured.

"I know," Carson replied, his eyes flicking to hers with a knowing smile. "Makes all this," he gestured vaguely towards the house, "seem less significant, don't you think?"

"Absolutely," she agreed. Her thoughts danced between the stars and the enigmatic man beside her. As much as she wanted to lose herself in the heavens above, Carson's presence was undeniably magnetic.

"Riley," he began softly, reaching for her hand, "I know tonight has been overwhelming, but I wanted to tell you how wonderful you've been. You're truly captivating." His thumb traced slow circles on her wrist, setting her nerves alight.

"Thank you," she whispered, her cheeks flushed with warmth. "You've made it easier."

"Anytime," he said, his voice low and seductive, his eyes never leaving hers.

In that moment, it was as if the world around them had ceased to exist. It was just Riley and Carson, two souls adrift in a sea of stars. The air seemed to crackle with anticipation, and before she could fully comprehend what was happening, Carson leaned in and pressed his lips against hers.

The kiss was tender, yet passionate, and Riley's thoughts scattered like stardust as she melted into his embrace. Her hands found their way to his broad shoulders, fingers digging into the fabric of his suit jacket as she lost herself in the delicious warmth of his touch.

When they finally broke apart, breathless and dazed, Riley couldn't help the euphoria that bubbled up within her. Her infatuation with Carson had grown exponentially in that single, stolen moment, and she knew there was no turning back.

"Wow," she whispered, still reeling from the intensity of their connection.

"Wow indeed," Carson agreed, his eyes dark and smoldering. "Shall we head back inside?"

"Of course," she replied, her mind still swimming in a haze of desire and wonder. As they turned to rejoin the party, Riley couldn't help but glance back at the stars one last time, silently thanking them for this unforgettable night.

Hand in hand, Riley and Carson stepped back into the opulent dining room filled with chatter and laughter. The party had clearly picked up in their absence, and for a moment, Riley felt like an outsider looking in.

"Welcome back," Ana, the President's wife, greeted them with a knowing smile. "I hope you two found the terrace to your liking."

"Absolutely stunning," Riley replied, trying to maintain composure. She couldn't help but feel that her cheeks were flushed from the kiss.

"Yes, it's lovely," Carson said smoothly, giving Ana a charming nod. Riley realized that she probably couldn't tell if he was ever being sincere or not – the artifice was incredibly convincing. Could she really trust a man like that? She quickly dismissed the thought.

Carson isn't Jake. Not every guy is like Jake.

The rest of the evening moved past like a blur, filled with moments of cocktails and small talk with people who loved being told how interesting they were. But even with the artificial veneer of it all, Riley felt her heart flutter every second that Carson was at her side.

Eventually the evening wound to a close, and she and Carson drove off, back into the cold night. The crisp air rushed through the open windows of the crossover as they left the fundraiser behind. Riley leaned her head back against the seat, enjoying the sensation of the wind flowing through her hair and caressing her cheeks.

"Thanks for inviting me out, Carson," she said, angled towards him with an appreciative smile.

"Of course, it's my pleasure" he responded, his eyes darting from the road to catch her gaze. "Did you manage to have a good time despite... you know?"

"The self involved rich people?" Riley laughed. "Absolutely. It's always amusing to meet people who are that certain of their own importance."

Carson chuckled, navigating a tight turn with ease. "I'm glad to hear that."

Silence settled between them, punctuated only by the hum of the engine and the rustle of leaves outside. Riley's thoughts drifted back to their moment on the terrace beneath the stars. A shiver ran down her spine, but not from the cold.

"Are you alright?" Carson asked, concern coloring his voice.

Riley shook herself out of her reverie, cheeks reddening. "Yeah, I'm fine. Just lost in thought."

"About anything in particular?" Carson pressed gently, clearly curious.

"About tonight," she admitted, meeting his eyes briefly before glancing away. "It was nice. I forgot what it's like to spend an evening at an elegant party. It's been far too long."

"Ah, yes. The glamor of being pimped out by your employer to milk money from millionaires," Carson grinned, a mischievous twinkle in his eye. "I'm glad you were with me too, Riley."

As they pulled up to Riley's house, she felt a surge of reluctance to leave Carson's company. She unbuckled her seatbelt and turned to face him. "Thank you. For everything."

"Anytime," he replied, his demeanor softening.

Riley hesitated for a moment before opening the door, her heart pounding in her chest. She stepped out and began making her way to the front porch, feeling Carson's presence behind her. When they reached the steps, Riley turned to face him once more.

"Goodnight, Carson," she whispered, her breath hitching as he leaned in.

"Goodnight, Riley," he murmured, his lips brushing against hers in a gentle kiss that sent shivers down her spine.

As they pulled apart, Riley felt a warmth spread through her chest, an unfamiliar feeling of happiness bubbling up inside her. She flashed him one last smile before heading inside, the memory of their shared kiss lingering on her lips.

Behind the closed door, she allowed herself a giddy giggle, fingers pressed to her still-tingling lips. For the first time in a long while, Riley Whittaker thought she might be falling for someone again.

Chapter 9

Mia locked the door to Markov Books and flipped the open sign to closed. The dim glow of the bookstore's reading lamps cast a warm light over Riley, Sarah, and Lucy as they huddled around an old wooden table in the back. The smell of musty old pages mixed with the faint scent of incense in the air. Mia's fingers traced the lines of a sigils etched into her left arm, a nervous habit she couldn't quite kick.

"So let's review what we know right now." Mia spoke in a hushed but urgent tone. "We know Emma was out at two different college bars the night she got turned – The Broken Inn and Swagger Jack's. We also know Sarah first spotted Daniel in those places when she started hunting him."

"And we're 100% certain Daniel didn't turn Emma?" Riley asked. "I just want to make sure we're not missing something obvious."

"Daniel had so little control over his vampiric energy that he could not even keep himself alive in sunlight for more than two minutes," Lucy said, shaking her head. "Making a new vampire is harder than the stories would lead you to believe, and he was not capable of it."

"Gotcha. Okay," Riley said. "I know it must have sounded like a stupid question, but I wanted to be sure."

"Not a stupid question," Sarah replied. "We can't know things unless we ask. If we don't, we just make decisions based on assumptions. That's how people get hurt."

Sarah gave Mia a look that made Mia more than a little uncomfortable.

"Okay, so here's the plan," Lucy began, her voice low and commanding, cutting through the rising tension. "We'll split up and head to those two bars. Keep your eyes open for any unusual behavior or the unnatural. At best we find signs of the Drake, but we may also find another vampire we can interrogate."

"Sounds simple enough," Sarah chimed in, her gaze lingering on Mia for a moment too long. The tension between them really was palpable, like the static charge before a storm. They still hadn't talked about the other night, and it was becoming clear to Mia that neither one of them wanted to actually broach the subject.

"Let's get this show on the road," Riley said, clapping her hands together. "Mia, you're with me. We'll take the first bar on the list."

As they stepped out of the bookstore and into the night, the distant hum of bass-heavy music throbbed through the air, a siren call leading them toward the bar district. Mia glanced at Riley, her best friend's silhouette framed by the flickering streetlights.

"So you doing okay?" Riley asked. "I figured you could probably use the space from Sarah."

"Yeah, thanks," Mia replied, as they walked down the street. "I've had a lot on my mind, and I think I'm at my limit."

"I mean, there's an evil vampire turning random people, and they're leaving corpses," Riley nodded. "It's a lot for anyone."

"Well, there's that and…" Mia paused. "Okay, this is going to sound dumb. One of the regulars at Markov Books, Nic? She's been obsessed with this tarot deck she ordered. She's been coming in multiple times a week to ask if its here yet. I called her this afternoon to let her know it shipped, right?

"Okay?" Riley responded.

"She's not answering her phone," Mia said quietly. "She was bugging me constantly, and then silence? It's weird."

"I'm sure she's fine, Mia," Riley said, trying to reassure her. "She probably just got busy."

"Yeah, probably." Mia tried to sound confident, but it wasn't working. "But she lives and works in this neighborhood."

"I get why you're worried, but let's not jump to conclusions, okay?" Riley put her hand on Mia's shoulder. "We can't do anything about it tonight, and we have a job to do. Don't get distracted."

"Right, let's keep our head in the game," Mia nodded. "Time to hunt."

As they approached the first venue, the steady pulse of music grew louder, vibrating through the soles of their feet. Pulling open the door to the Broken Inn, the overwhelming smell of sweaty desperate bodies and the wall of sound overwhelmed the senses. It was the worst kind of college bar – half the people here were likely using fake IDs, and the sticky texture of spilled beer clung to almost every surface.

As the two walked up to the bar, Riley's phone buzzed with an incoming text. She glanced at the screen and smirked as her phone lit up her face. Mia leaned in, her curiosity piqued.

"Who's texting you?" Mia asked, her voice sharpening with annoyance.

"Carson," Riley replied nonchalantly, tapping out a response with one hand while waiving down the bartender with the other. "God, I still need to tell you how the other night went."

Riley's phone buzzed again, and she blushed a little. She started tapping out another reply.

"Seriously, Riley? We're supposed to be hunting vampires, not flirting with the hot history department head," Mia said with mild exasperation. "And you warned *me* about being distracted?"

"Relax, it's just a text. It's not like I'm blowing off the mission," Riley defended herself, somehow deftly signaling the bartender to bring her a whiskey. A glass materialized in front of her in short order.

Mia clenched her jaw, frustration creeping under her skin. She scanned the bar for any signs of vampire activity, the murmur of conversation and laughter blending into an indistinct hum around her. Her thoughts churned with irritation, the delicate balance of focus and control threatening to crumble.

****

Lucy and Sarah moved through the dimly lit space of Swagger Jack's like shadows, their eyes flickering over patrons in search of their prey. The scent of stale beer clung to the air, mingling with the sweet tang of artificial fog from the dance floor.

"Interesting choice of hunting grounds," Sarah remarked, her words laced with suspicion. "Was ordering

91

me a drink necessary camouflage, or are you just trying to get me drunk?"

"Can't it be both?" Lucy replied coyly, her crimson lips curving into a seductive smile. "Besides, you can learn a lot about someone by how they behave when their inhibitions are lowered."

"Is that what this is? An attempt to loosen my tongue?" Sarah countered sharply, her defenses rising like a fortress wall.

"Perhaps," Lucy admitted, her gaze lingering on Sarah's lips for a moment too long. "Or maybe I just don't want us to stick out like sore thumbs."

Sarah raised an eyebrow, her distrust of Lucy obvious to anyone who happened to look. But Sarah knew better than to let her personal feelings get in the way of getting a job done. "Focus, Lucy," Sarah admonished. "We're here for a reason."

"Of course," Lucy agreed, her voice smooth as silk. "But it doesn't hurt to have a little fun along the way, does it?"

"In my experience, finding the 'fun' in any of this is a great way to get people hurt," Sarah answered. "Especially me."

The bass from the pounding music reverberated through Sarah's chest as she scanned the bar, her eyes flicking from one face to another like a predator sizing up potential prey.

"Tell me, Sarah," Lucy began, her voice a velvety purr that somehow cut through the cacophony of drunken laughter and clinking glasses. "What brought you back to Mia? Your hunt brought you to this town, but sleeping with her again... was it love or something more selfish?"

Sarah's grip tightened around the edge of the bar, the hard edge biting into her skin. "Why do you care?"

"Curiosity, perhaps," Lucy replied, her eyes gleaming with predatory intent. "Or maybe I just want to know what makes you tick."

"Maybe I just missed her," Sarah said defensively. "Is that so hard to believe?"

"Forgive me, but when I'm taking on an adversary like the Drake, histories like yours and Mia's can make things… complicated," Lucy responded, her fingertips dancing along the rim of her glass.

"Complicated is an understatement," Sarah muttered under her breath, the bitterness lingering on her tongue like a poison.

"Then enlighten me," Lucy challenged, her gaze locked onto Sarah's, unyielding and hungry for information. Sarah looked at Lucy and felt like she was staring at an alluring tiger, and she was the prey.

****

Mia's eyes darted between the patrons of the Broken Inn, searching for any signs of unusual behavior. Her senses were heightened, attuned to the slightest hint of danger lurking beneath the surface.

"See anything suspicious yet?" Riley asked, breaking the silence as she sipped her whiskey.

"Nothing yet," Mia admitted, her fingers tapping a restless rhythm on the table. "But something feels off. I just can't put my finger on it."

"Maybe it's just paranoia," Riley suggested, glancing back at her phone. "We've been on edge for so long that everything seems suspicious."

"Or maybe we're just getting closer to finding them," Mia countered, her determination unwavering despite the gnawing doubt clawing at the edges of her mind. "We can't afford to let our guard down, Riley. Not now."

"Agreed," Riley replied, nodding in apparent agreement. It was strange how a place like this changed from inviting to dangerous just depending on how you looked at it. The dim, amber glow of the bar lights could be both intimate or eerie depending on your state of mind. The bar's patrons drank and laughed, blissfully unaware of the danger lurking beneath the surface. Mia's fingers drummed impatiently on the worn wooden table, her eyes never leaving the crowd. In her mind, every unfamiliar face was a potential threat.

"Any chance they're just not out tonight?" Riley asked, feigning nonchalance as she snuck another glance at her phone screen. Mia tried to hide her frustration, but Riley's obvious split attention was infuriating.

"Possible... but unlikely. That many vampires means someone must always be looking to feed," Mia murmured, the words barely audible above the cacophony of clinking glasses and drunken laughter. Her voice was tinged with frustration, both at their lack of success and Riley's lack of focus.

Riley nodded, but it was increasingly clear what was on her phone was more important to her right now than the situation at hand. Mia had never seen Riley get so caught up in someone like this, and under normal circumstances Mia'd be happy for her. But right now? At this minute?

It really sucked.

"Riley, I think I've got something," Mia suddenly whispered, her gaze locked on a tall, pale figure who seemed to glide effortlessly through the throng of swaying bodies. His eyes were dark pools, devoid of emotion, and his movements were unnaturally fluid, almost predatory. Sure, he *could* just be some weird goth guy, but something about him made a sigil on the back of her neck begin to buzz.

"Finally," Riley muttered under her breath, tearing herself away from her phone. She visibly shook as she caught sight of the man Mia was watching. Something about him screamed danger, and it wasn't his all-black attire or the eerie grace with which he moved. "Yeah, the goth dude is pretty creepy."

"Follow my lead," Mia instructed, her voice low and urgent. She rose from her seat, her body tense with anticipation as she prepared to confront the suspected vampire. Riley nodded, hastily grabbing her phone off of the table.

Stay focused, Mia mentally chided herself in almost an echo of Sarah's voice, feeling a sudden surge of adrenaline as they moved closer to their target. The scent of his cologne filled her nostrils, a heady mix of cedarwood and something darker, more sinister that she couldn't quite identify.

"Let's do this," Riley whispered, casting one last glance at Mia before they followed the enigmatic stranger outside.

The cool night air brushed against Mia's skin, heightening her senses as she scanned the dark alley for any sign of their quarry. Riley followed closely behind, her breath ragged and uneven, betraying her nervousness. The shadows cast by the dim streetlights seemed alive, writhing and shifting like a living organism, giving the scene an eerie, otherworldly quality.

"Shit, where did he go. Keep your eyes peeled," Mia whispered, her voice barely audible over the distant murmur of laughter and music drifting from the bar. She felt a knot of frustration forming in her chest, her patience wearing thin as they ventured further into the darkness.

"Got it," Riley muttered, her gaze darting between the shadows and her phone screen, which flashed with another incoming message.

"Riley, focus!" Mia hissed, her eyes narrowing as she spotted a fleeting glimpse of their target disappearing around a corner. She clenched her fists, her nails digging into her palms as she fought the urge to lash out at her friend. She moved in quiet pursuit of the figure, with Riley close behind. As they rounded the corner, the man ducked into shadows, and Mia struggled to keep up.

"Sorry, just one second," Riley mumbled, her thumbs tapping away furiously on her phone as she sent a brief response, catching Mia's attention. When she turned around, the figure was gone. This was the straw that broke the camel's back.

"Unbelievable," Mia muttered under her breath, her irritation bubbling over as she desperately tried to figure out where the potential vampire had gone. A strangled noise of frustration escaped her lips as she turned to face Riley, who was still absorbed in her conversation with Carson.

"Are you kidding me right now?" Mia snapped, her anger flaring as she snatched the phone from Riley's grasp. "We had something, and you blew it because you couldn't put your damn phone down for five minutes!"

"Hey, give that back!" Riley protested, her cheeks flushed with embarrassment as she reached for her phone. But Mia held it out of reach, her expression a mixture of disappointment and fury.

"The stakes are so high right now, and you're acting like a teenager," Mia growled, tossing the phone back to Riley storming away from the alley. They'd missed an opportunity to uncover more about the Drake's plans because Riley couldn't concentrate on the task at hand.

"Where are you going?" Riley called after her, but Mia didn't bother to respond. Her anger had reached its boiling point, and all she wanted was answers – or at least a better understanding of the forces they were up against.

"I'm going to see if I can pick up his trail," she muttered to herself, quickening her pace as she navigated the dark streets, her anger fueling her determination. One thing was certain: Mia wasn't about to let another opportunity slip through her fingers.

****

"I think this is a dead end," Sarah said, looking to Lucy.

"It seems like it might be," Lucy sighed. "But we should see this through. We're limited in the leads we have. Perhaps we could spend this time becoming more acquainted with each other?"

Sarah looked at Lucy, and tried not to react. In her experience, vampires were violent, dangerous things that preyed on the defenseless, but Mia kept assuring Sarah that it wasn't true. The idea that "most" vampires didn't go around hurting people didn't match her lived experience, though Sarah had to admit that the only ones who *would* show up on her radar were the ones willing to drop bodies.

If you only ever encountered the killers, how would you know any of the others existed to begin with?

"Fine, you want to play twenty-questions, go for it," Sarah replied, finally starting on the drink she'd been carrying around untouched.

"So from what I gather from Mia, you are also a witch?" Lucy asked carefully. "I intend no offense, but you don't exactly strike me as one."

"I don't consider myself one anymore, no," Sarah responded. "I don't know how much Mia's told you about

our past, but two years ago I lost my ability to use magic –
and I have no interest in getting it back."

"That seems… drastic?" Lucy said quietly, leaning
closer to Sarah. Her movements were as fluid as liquid
mercury, and likely just as dangerous. "Do you miss it at
all?"

"I honestly don't think I do. Part of me misses what I
did with that magic though, and I hate that I miss that,"
Sarah said, almost getting lost in memory. "It's
complicated."

"Life often is," Lucy smiled, putting her hand gently on
her arm. "Is there a reason you can't use magic anymore?"

"A pretty big one," Sarah sighed. "Connecting to magic
is done through the soul, and I only have roughly half of
one these days."

"I won't ask you how you lost it," Lucy said, shifting in
her seat. "I can't see any circumstances where that would be
a happy memory."

"It most definitely isn't," Sarah whispered. She took a
sip from her drink, and the two sat in silence for a moment.

"You want to know something almost ironic? Neither
one of us is has come out with the right sum on that front,"
Lucy said with a small smile. "You have half a soul, and
I'm cursed with a second. Neither one of us able to truly
live like the rest of humanity."

Sarah blinked, "I'm sorry, what? Two souls?"

"My dear," Lucy said, sitting back slightly. "Has no one
explained to you how vampires work?"

"Mia was always the one in search of lore and theory,"
Sarah said shaking her head. "I was always just interested
in what I could do. I read recipes, Mia wrote them."

"What I'm telling you isn't a secret, and I am confident
Mia knows it," Lucy explained. "It's been understood by
occult scholars, ceremonial magicians and you modern

witches for quite some time. Vampirism is a form of possession."

Sarah recoiled in disgust, "You're a demon."

"I am *not* a demon, Sarah," Lucy shook her head. "I, the person who is talking, was born a human and I have a human soul. The thing that possesses me is not a demon either. It's something that doesn't have a firm category – but we call it the 'vampiric spirit.'"

"And what is the 'vampiric spirit,'" Sarah said, eyes narrowing.

"It's an ancient thing… some say older than demons," Lucy said. "It can't control a person, or subvert their will. If it enters someone, it doesn't take over… but it has instincts that the person will feel. The hunger vampires experience… it comes from the spirit. But the person still decides whether or not to surrender to it. The person makes the decision to kill."

Sarah just listened, continuing to sip her drink.

"All of our powers and weaknesses come from the spirit," Lucy continued. "A vampire can't go into daylight because the vampiric spirit is vulnerable to the sun. I can walk in daylight not because of some grand power, but because I have learned to *suppress* the thing that makes me a monster."

"If it's just possession, couldn't you cure a vampire with an exorcism?" Sarah asked, puzzling it out.

"No," Lucy said, shaking her head. "Unlike demons, the vampiric spirit holds tight. It's a survivor. Many have tried, but none have ever managed to succeed. So we continue on, living."

"Sounds difficult, to manage something like that every day," Sarah said quietly. "Always worried that you'll hurt the ones you love around you."

Sarah never thought she'd relate this much to a vampire.

****

Mia navigated the darkened streets of Parrish Mills, searching desperately for the man she'd seen at the bar. She ran down the sidewalk in an almost artful dance, avoiding the crunch of leaves and other obstacles that might reveal her pursuit. But after turning yet another corner, she realized the search would be fruitless.

It had been half an hour, the man must be long gone.

Mia stopped to catch her breath. Frustration overtook her, and without thinking she kicked a nearby fire hydrant, badly stubbing her toe through her boot.

"Fuck!" Mia yelled, hopping over to a nearby bench. She sat down, and quickly pulled off her boot to inspect the damage. "So many spells, but none are 'protection against fire hydrants.'"

Leaning back on the bench, Mia realized she was sitting on some sort of flier. Pulling it out from under her, the words "Brotherhood of the Eternal Light" were emblazoned across the top. Rolling her eyes, Mia crumpled the piece of paper into a ball, and tossed it into a nearby trash can.

Dejectedly, Mia walked back to where she'd parked her truck, ready to drive home. Pulling herself into the rusty red Ford Ranger, she sighed as she slid the key into the ignition.

And then she saw him.

Tall and moving incredibly unnaturally, the man from the bar walked directly by Mia's truck, not even seeming to acknowledge or notice her presence. The sigil on the back of her neck seemed to scream at her.

This was some sort of unnatural being. Mia was certain of it. The man climbed onto a motorcycle, and drove off into the night.

Mia put the truck in gear, and followed closely behind.

Chapter 10

The full moon cast an eerie glow on the dilapidated church on the edge of town, its cracked and crumbling stone walls standing as a testament to the passage of time. Mia put the truck in park, and watched the tall man climb off his bike and go inside. She closed the door to her Ranger as quietly as possible, and approached the building cautiously, her boots crunching on the gravel path.

"Seriously?" She muttered under her breath, rolling her eyes. "An abandoned church? Talk about clichés…"

As she neared the entrance, the tattoo on the back of Mia's neck began to tingle. She took a deep breath, feeling the familiar thrill of adrenaline rush through her veins, and stepped into the shadows.

Mia peered through a crack in the heavy wooden doors, surveying the scene before her. The nave was filled with an assortment of mismatched chairs, tables and old pews, while candles spread across the space flickered wildly providing the only light. The air was thick with the scent of blood and decay, and she could see figures moving inside, but she wasn't sure how many. It didn't sound like a small crowd though.

Alright, Mia, you're doing recon, she thought, suppressing her rising anxiety and trying to keep her head in the game. *You're not here to fight, you're here to gather information.*

Mia's heart pounded in her chest as she considered the best approach to watch and observe. Staying by the door was not an option, since she had no idea if anyone else would be showing up or going out. She knew she was outnumbered and outmatched, but she couldn't afford to hesitate.

Sneaking around to the side of the church, Mia spotted a side door half off of its hinges. Carefully placing it aside, Mia snuck into a back hall of the dilapidated building.

Don't screw this up Mia, Mia thought silently. Getting caught by over a dozen vampires would be very, very bad for her. Moving down the dark hall, she found a narrow set of stairs leading up into darkness. *In for a penny...*

Mia climbed the steps, trying to be as silent as possible. As she reached the top, she found herself standing in a balcony behind the altar, overlooking the church nave. Mia stayed low, trying not to draw attention.

Okay, time to play 'count the assholes,' she thought sarcastically, focusing on the details of the scene before her. Her eyes darted around the space, making a conscious note of their numbers and positions; twelve scattered amongst the pews, three near the altar, and another three skulking in the shadows by the confessional booth.

Eighteen, she thought, cursing internally. This wasn't going to be easy, but she had no choice – she needed to find out what these things were up to and put an end to it.

A flicker of movement caught Mia's eye, drawing her gaze to a huddle of newly turned vampires. *Three more. Twenty-one.* Among them, she spotted a familiar silhouette with distinctive, bright purple hair: Nic. Mia's heart lurching with a mixture of anger and protectiveness. The sight of her friend standing there amidst the undead predators, skin pale and eyes hollow, sent a shiver down Mia's spine.

She had just seen her a few days ago in the shop, and here Nic was, one of the Drake's new vampires.

"Dammit, Nic," Mia muttered under her breath, clenching her fists in frustration. "What the hell did you get yourself into?"

Mia tried to make it to the edge of the balcony and get a better look, but the floor beneath her began to buckle, her boot punching through the broken wood with a sickening crack. The sound cracked like thunder, ringing throughout the abandoned church. Every single head in the building turned, their eyes all locked on Mia.

For a moment the vampires all just stared at her, and she just stared back. It seemed as though it had never occurred to any of those gathered that someone might break in, and none of them were sure what to actually do now that Mia had.

"So, uh, hi?" Mia said nervously, pulling her leg out of the hole in the floor and giving a meek wave. The tension seemed to hold, and for a brief moment Mia almost believed she could just slowly back out of there.

"Get her!" a voice yelled, and the church erupted into chaos. Mia had to act fast if she was going to survive.

"Alright," she whispered, her voice barely audible even to herself, "Time for creative solutions." There was an ornate chandelier hanging above the congregation. Mia traced the cables suspending it to the north wall, and quickly activated a series of sigils on her forearms.

"Here goes nothing," she muttered, casting a final glance at Nic before activating the spell.

An arc of energy flowed out of Mia's right arm, bouncing along multiple surfaces until it reached the supports, snapping them and sending the large, metal chandelier crashing into a number of the vampires below.

Mia leapt from the edge, vaulting over the railing, and onto the altar as several vampires reached the top of the stairs to the balcony she'd previously occupied.

"Damn, I should've brought sunglasses," Mia muttered under her breath as she prepared to cast another spell. The incantation rolled off her tongue with practiced ease, her fingers tracing a small rune on her side.

The moment the final syllable left her lips, the church erupted in a searing burst of light. It was as if a thousand suns had converged upon the ancient pews and stained glass windows, bathing everything in an unbearable radiance. The vampires shrieked and hissed, shielding their sensitive eyes as they recoiled from the unexpected onslaught.

It wouldn't hurt them like sunlight, but these vampires were apparently too new to know that.

"Enjoy the show, chucklefucks," Mia said under her breath, smirking despite the tension coiling in her chest. She darted forward, using the chaos to her advantage as she weaved through the crowd of disoriented creatures.

"Mia! Watch out for the —" a voice cried out, as an arm grabbed Mia and pushed her out of the way of a crashing pew thrown by one of the vampires. Mia looked turned and was face to face with Nic, who now had shards of the shattered wood sticking out of her shoulder. "You need to get out of here, now! Let's go!"

"I don't think your friends are going to let me, Nic," Mia replied. She braced herself, muscles coiled like springs as the vampires approached. Their fangs gleamed menacingly, hunger and malice radiating from each predatory step. Mia's heart raced, sweat beading on her brow, but she refused to let fear control her.

"Alright, kiddos," she taunted, her voice laced with defiance. "Who wants to dance first?"

The vampires lunged, their movements swift and lethal. Mia met them head-on, her body a whirlwind of motion as she ducked and weaved through their attacks. She could feel the sharp sting of claws grazing her skin as she barely avoided their blows.

Mia was suddenly incredibly grateful for having the foresight to incorporate protection against this sort of thing into the spells that marked her body.

"Keep moving, Mia," she chastised herself, gritting her teeth as she narrowly avoided another swipe. Her mind raced, searching for any advantage to exploit against her supernatural foes. They might not be able to bite her, but her sigils wouldn't do anything against them trying to beat her to death.

"Nic, you need to try and make your way to the exit," she instructed, her voice strained but determined.

"Okay, but what about you?" Nic's concern was evident, even in the midst of chaos.

"Trust me, Nic," Mia replied, a smirk playing at the corners of her mouth. "I'll be right behind you."

Mia's fingers danced over her tattoos, activating the ones that snaked across her right arm and left thigh. She traced the intricate patterns as she muttered an incantation under her breath. Her body hummed with energy, each symbol glowing with a fierce, otherworldly light.

"Guess it's finally time to see what these things can really do in a fight," she murmured to herself, a wicked smile curving her lips.

With a flourish of her hands, she unleashed a torrent of arcane energies, the air crackling and shimmering around her. The nearest vampires recoiled, hissing in pain and confusion as the intense magic assaulted their senses. Mia seized the opportunity, darting forward as fast as she could.

Mia threw a punch, her now glowing fist connecting with bone-crushing force. A sickening crunch echoed through the church as the vampire's jaw shattered, its head snapping back at an unnatural angle.

God, I hope that hurt as much as it sounded like it did, Mia thought, allowing herself a brief moment of satisfaction before turning her attention to the next adversary. This was the first time she'd put most of these spells into practice, and it was nice to see they worked as planned.

As the battle raged on, the scent of sweat and blood filled the air – a potent, intoxicating mixture that fueled the frenzy of the undead horde. The improvised spells Mia used to enhance her strength and speed were burning out fast. Mia found herself tiring, her muscles burning from the relentless onslaught. She hadn't charged up for a fight, and she was burning out fast.

"Come on, Graves. You've faced worse than this," she lied, mentally berating herself for her flagging stamina. She braced herself for the worst, knowing she had hardly any magic left in her. The horde of vampires descended upon her like a pack of rabid animals, their strength and hunger washing over her like an oppressive tide.

"Let's go!" Nic shouted, grabbing hold of Mia's hand and pulling her through the frenzied melee of snarling vampires.

A vampire tackled Nic, slamming her into a wooden pew, sending it shattering. Mia pulled Nic to her feat, and unleashed a ball of energy sending the vampire across the room. Nic was definitely looking worse for wear, and her clothes were slick with blood.

"Let's move, c'mon," Mia said, her breath ragged. As they raced towards the exit, the world around them seemed to blur into a nightmare of crimson-tinged shadows and monstrous shapes. The cold air stung Mia's lungs with each ragged breath, but she refused to slow down – not when freedom was finally within their grasp.

"Almost there," Nic panted, her grip on Mia's hand tightening. "Just a little further!"

And then, just as suddenly as it had begun, the chaos was behind them. They burst out of the church and into the night, the vampires close in pursuit. Out of breath, Mia and Nic jumped into Mia's beat up Ford Ranger. She hit the gas and sped off into the darkness, leaving their attackers behind them.

"Looks like we lost them," Mia murmured, her heart still hammering wildly against her ribs. "For now, anyway."

"Thank God," Nic sighed, collapsing in the passenger seat, staring out the window at the starless sky. "What were you even doing there, Mia?"

"Almost getting killed because I'm an idiot," Mia replied "How did you even end up getting mixed up with that crowd."

"It wasn't by choice - they grabbed me the other night, and I woke up in that church the next day," Nic said, her voice wavering as she clutched at a wound on her stomach. "But Mia... I think there's something you should know."

"Save it for later," Mia insisted, her chest tightening with unspoken dread. "Let's just focus on getting out of here first, okay?"

"Okay," Nic whispered, her eyes glistening with unshed tears. "It can wait."

"Good," Mia said, forcing a smile onto her face as they prepared to make their escape. "Now let's get moving before our luck runs out."

Mia pulled over a few miles away so she could stop and dress her wounds, as the adrenaline was wearing off. She was suddenly aware of the cuts and bruises all over her body, wincing as she climbed out onto the side of the country road.

The sickly-sweet smell of blood and sweat hung heavy in the air, mingling with the damp earth beneath them. Mia's breath came in ragged gasps, her lungs burning as she scanned their surroundings for any lurking danger.

"Are you… safe?" Nic's voice trembled, her breathing labored as she leaned against the side of the truck for support.

"Seems so," Mia replied, her eyes never leaving the darkness around them. "For now, at least." She couldn't shake the feeling that these vampires wouldn't give up so easily. They needed to keep moving.

"Hey," Mia said softly, turning her attention to Nic. "You did great back there, you know. I'm really proud of you."

"Thanks," Nic replied weakly, offering her a weary smile. "I couldn't let them hurt you, Mia."

"So I have this friend I want you to meet, she can help–," Mia started, before setting her eyes on Nic's pale face and bloodied clothes. "Nic, are you okay? You took quite a beating back there."

"Never better," Nic lied, her voice cracking as she winced in pain. "Just need a little rest, is all."

"Nic–" Mia started, but stopped abruptly when she noticed the crimson stain spreading across Nic's sweater. "Oh my god, you're hurt bad."

"Really? I hadn't noticed," Nic replied through gritted teeth, her sarcasm failing to mask the agony in her expression. She collapsed to the ground, hitting it with a sickening thud.

"Damn it, Nic!" Mia snapped, dropping to her knees beside her friend. Her hands hovered over the wound, a large piece of wood still protruding from it. "Why didn't you tell me sooner?"

"Didn't want you to worry," Nic whispered, her eyes beginning to glaze over. "Besides, you had more important problems. I needed to get you out of there."

"You're important too," Mia insisted fiercely, tears pricking at the corners of her eyes. She knew she didn't have much time. "You're my friend."

"Hey, Mia" Nic murmured, her breaths coming in short, shallow gasps. "Just promise me you'll be okay, alright?"

"Please don't say that," Mia begged, her voice breaking as she cradled Nic's face in her hands. "Don't you dare give up on me now! You're a vampire, you should be able to heal yourself!"

"I'm sorry," Nic choked out, her body trembling with the effort to stay conscious. "I just...can't hold on any longer. They told me I can't heal without feeding, and I don't want to hurt anyone else. They made me feed once already and I can't do that to a person again."

"Nic, no!" Mia cried, her vision blurred with tears as she clung desperately to her friend. "You're just a kid! I can… I can give you some of my blood… you'll be okay, I can make this okay…"

"Hey, it's fine, Mia" Nic whispered, her voice barely audible as her strength drained away. "I kept you safe and that's all that matters."

"You matter too, god damn it..." Mia sobbed, her heart shattering into a thousand pieces as Nic's body went limp in her arms. Every one of Mia's muscles were on fire, but it was nothing compared to the pain in her heart right now.

****

Mia's bloodied hand trembled as she grasped the cold brass doorknob, each ounce of strength mustered to push the heavy door open. She stumbled into Lucy's dimly-lit Victorian house, her exhaustion palpable. The scent of burning candles and ancient leather filled her nostrils as her body screamed in agony from the battle at the church. Her once pristine black skirt and tank top clung to her body like a second skin, soaked with sweat and blood.

"Lucy! Sarah! Riley! Anyone!" Mia called out, her voice cracking from the strain of her injuries. Each breath felt like inhaling shards of glass, tearing at her lungs. Her legs crumbled under her weight, sending her tumbling onto the cool hardwood floor.

"Oh my lord, what happened to you?" Lucy materialized by Mia's side like a phantom, her eyes wide with concern. The 300-year-old vampire had probably seen her fair share of carnage, but Mia was looking rough.

Sarah bolted into the room, the anger in her eyes melted away into fear as she took in the sight of Mia, battered and broken on the floor. Riley was close behind, staring in abject shock.

"Oh, Mia," Sarah breathed, her voice laden with worry.

"Nice to see you too," Mia grunted, attempting to inject a semblance of sarcasm into her pained words. "I swear I only fucked up a little, and most of this blood isn't mine."

"Let's get you off this floor and onto something more comfortable," Lucy said, looping one arm under Mia's shoulder while Riley supported her from the other side. Together, they helped the injured witch to a nearby couch, its plush cushions welcoming her like a loving embrace.

"Is it too soon to ask for a sponge bath?" Mia quipped weakly as she sank into the couch, her eyelids fluttering shut for a moment. She couldn't afford to rest just yet; there was too much at stake.

"Focus, Mia," Sarah chided gently, her hand brushing back a strand of hair from Mia's sweaty forehead. "Tell us what happened."

"So, uh, I found a lead?" Mia squeaked out, wincing in pain. "I swear I felt better earlier, but the adrenaline seems to have worn off now..."

"I thought you were going off to mope," Riley said, holding Mia's hand. "This is all my fault."

"It's not your fault, and I kinda was," Mia sighed. "But then I got 'lucky?' I saw the vampire we spotted at the bar and followed him to an abandoned church outside of town. He, uh, had some friends there."

"So you decided to get the shit kicked out of you?" Sarah replied. "What were you thinking going somewhere like that alone? What's rule number one!"

"Always bring a buddy," Mia said weakly. "Really wish you'd been there. It's going to take a good eight hours to recharge all the spells I burned through in a few minutes. But hey, I finally know that most of them work."

"You're not allowed to get hurt like this," Riley said. "You're supposed to be tough and strong so we can go out drinking and tell each other all our secrets."

"I'll keep that in mind," Mia sighed, her eyes welled with tears. "Riley... Nic was there. They turned her. She saved me, but... she didn't make it out."

"Oh my god, Mia," Riley gasped.

"Most of these wounds are superficial," Lucy said, quietly. "Do you have the necessary magic to heal them?"

"I will in the morning," Mia replied. "I think I just need some sleep, like a full day's rest. There were like two dozen vampires at the church. It's the one off Ferry street? It was a bit on fire when I left, so I don't think they'll stay there."

"I'll go in the morning and see if they're still there," Sarah said in a determined tone. "If they are, there will be repercussions for this."

"I'm going to get you home," Riley said quietly. "Then you're going to call Bobbi, and she's going to keep you in bed all day and that's final."

"But..."

"No buts, Mia," Riley said. "Just your ass in bed."

"Heal yourself, Graves," Sarah said, her voice cold as steel. "There's a lot more fight left for all of us."

Chapter 11

Riley slid into the velvet embrace of a high-backed booth, her eyes sparkling with mischief as they settled on Carson Smith. No vampires or Mia drama tonight – just a hot guy and good food that Riley wouldn't have to pay for. Should she really be spending an evening like this in the current state of her world? Probably not. But Mia needed to rest anyway, so they wouldn't be taking any action for the time being anyway.

The dimly lit restaurant was illuminated with the soft glow of candlelight and the faint scent of roses. As Carson took his seat across from Riley, she couldn't help but let loose a playful smirk.

"Seriously, Carson? You're took me to 'La Petite Château?'" Her voice dripped with sarcasm. "I thought we agreed on something low-key."

Carson leaned forward, his eyes dancing with amusement. "Well, you know what they say – go big or go home. Besides, I wanted to impress you with my impeccable taste in overpriced French cuisine."

"Ah, yes. Nothing says 'I'm a man of culture' quite like the restaurant all the high schoolers try to take their prom dates to," Riley retorted, rolling her eyes playfully as she picked up a menu.

"Exactly," he replied with a grin, matching her sarcastic tone. "You know, there's a certain je ne sais quoi about a French restaurant whose chef is from Paris... Texas."

"Now now, I heard he just studied there, I heard he's actually from Marseilles... Illinois," she countered, her laughter bubbling up between them.

As they perused the menu, Riley noted the weight of the parchment-like paper, feeling the crisp texture beneath her fingertips. It had been a long time since someone had taken her out to a nice dinner, and she was enjoying every moment of it, regardless of how cheesy the setting.

"I've heard good things about the duck à l'orange?" Carson suggested, breaking the silence.

"I've never really been one for duck," Riley replied thoughtfully. "I was thinking about the steak frites."

"Ah, so you're a meat and potatoes kind of girl," he said, his eyes crinkling at the corners as he flashed her a charming smile. "I can appreciate that."

As they chatted and flirted over glasses of rich red wine, their banter flowed as smoothly as the velvety liquid itself. The notes of sarcasm and teasing seemed to dance in harmony with the delicate strains of a violin that drifted through the room. The more time they spent together, the more Riley found herself drawn to Carson's easy charisma and wit.

"Here's to second dates that don't involve dive bars," she declared, raising her glass in a toast.

"Or that happen at all," he added with a grin, clinking his glass against hers. Carson leaned in closer, his voice a low purr, "I have to admit, Riley... I've never met anyone quite as amazing as you."

His words fanned a warm blush across her cheeks, and she glanced down at her plate, trying to suppress a smile.

"You don't say? Well, flattery will get you everywhere, Dr. Smith."

"I mean, it's impossible to deny. I looked you up, you know," he replied, his fingers brushing against hers, sending shivers up her spine. "I read your paper on 'Political Movements and the Cult of Personality in the 20th Century' – it was quite insightful. I only understood about half of it, but I loved what I did."

"You read that of all things?" she asked incredulously. "That got published in the most mid of mid-tier journals. No one read that."

"The way you write about these things shows a firmer understanding of social dynamics and power than anyone I've ever met," Carson said, with a smile. "I don't know how to explain how humbling it was to explore a topic I thought I thoroughly understood and learn that I was still but a journeyman."

"You study *what* things happened, while I study *why* things happen," Riley smiled. "And if you think that repeatedly telling me how brilliant I am is going to get me to come home with you… well keep going and we'll find out."

"I might just do that," Carson winked.

As they shared a dessert of rich chocolate mousse, Riley couldn't shake the feeling that something was off. It prickled at the back of her mind like an itch she couldn't quite reach. Everything about Carson seemed too good to be true. No one could be this perfect, could they? Was the same blindspot that had made her miss what a jerk Jake was affecting her judgment here too?

"Are you alright, Riley?" Carson asked, his concern evident in his dark eyes. "You seem a bit preoccupied."

"Sorry, I'm just..." She shook her head, attempting to dismiss her apprehension. "I've had some bad relationships in the past – I don't want to talk about my baggage, but you honestly just seem too good to be real."

"Then allow me to assure you, I am very much real," he said, grinning as he offered her another spoonful of mousse. "And you've always deserved better. I think you deserve the world itself."

Riley laughed and accepted the sweet indulgence, savoring the rich taste as it melted on her tongue. Yet even as she enjoyed the dessert and Carson's undeniable charm, that nagging feeling persisted. Despite her instincts, Riley found herself captivated by Carson's charisma though, unable to resist the magnetic pull of his presence.

And she couldn't resist the invitation of a night cap at his home a few blocks away.

The cool evening air nipped at Riley's cheeks as she and Carson stepped out of the restaurant, the warm glow of its interior giving way to the dimly lit street. The click-clack of her heels echoed through the night, making it feel like they were the only two people in the world. Carson, ever the gentleman, offered his arm for support as they made their way towards his home.

"Now I don't want any funny business from you" Riley asked, her voice wavering slightly. "I'm not the kind of girl who usually goes home with a person on the second date."

"Then I shall be absolutely lacking in humor or professionalism," Carson replied with an easy smile. "I merely want to get the legendary Riley Whittaker's opinion on my taste in whiskey."

Riley forced a laugh, nodding in agreement. But inside, her anxiety swirled like a dark storm cloud.

As they approached his elegant townhouse, Riley's heart hammered in her chest, her body tense with anticipation. The flickering street lamps cast deep shadows on the brick facade, their playful dance belying the dread that had settled in her stomach. This was either the best or worst decision she could be making right now.

"Here we are," Carson announced, fumbling with his keys before unlocking the front door. The heavy oak swung open, revealing a tastefully decorated living room bathed in soft lamplight.

"Wow," breathed Riley, her eyes drinking in the sophisticated surroundings. "Your place is gorgeous."

"Thank you," he said, closing the door behind them. "Make yourself at home."

Riley hesitated, then removed her coat and draped it over a nearby chair. As Carson disappeared deeper into the home to fetch their drinks, she wandered around the room, admiring the ornate furnishings and exquisite artwork. Almost everything in the room was an antique, and Riley swore she'd seen the painting over the fireplace in a museum before.

"Here you are," Carson said, reappearing with two glasses of whiskey in hand. Startled, Riley jumped back, her heart racing at his sudden presence.

"Sorry, I didn't mean to frighten you," he apologized, offering her a glass.

"Th-thanks," she stammered, taking a sip to steady her nerves.

"So you'll have to tell me what you think of this," Carson said. "It's from a small distillery I visited in Scotland a few years ago. It's an 18 year old single malt."

As Riley drank the scotch, she began to explain her extensive opinions on whiskey, Carson sat with rapt attention, hanging on to her every word. He really did seem to be genuinely interested in what she thought, which was a strange change of pace. If she had said anything like this to Mia, she'd probably get a stare of polite boredom in response.

As she continued, Riley couldn't help but notice a strange draft, its icy tendrils sending shivers down her spine. The source to a seemed to be coming from an innocuous bookcase. Riley crossed the room to inspect it, her fingers brushing against the spines of leather-bound tomes.

"Carson, do you feel that?" she asked, her voice barely above a whisper.

"Feel what?" he replied, joining her by the bookcase.

"Like a breeze, coming from..." Her sentence trailed off as her hand inadvertently pressed a hidden latch, causing the bookcase to swing open and reveal a secret room beyond.

"Riley, wait!" Carson cried out, his eyes wide with panic. But it was too late – the truth lay exposed before her, like a serpent ready to strike.

Within the hidden chamber, a macabre collection of relics and artifacts adorned the walls, each one more chilling than the last. In the center, an ominous stone altar stood sentinel, its surface stained with dark crimson.

Blood. The stains were blood.

Riley's heart pounded in her chest like a wild animal caught in a trap, each frantic beat screaming at her to run. The cold air from the hidden room whispered sinister secrets into her ear, chilling her to the bone. Her breath came in ragged gasps as she stared at the twisted relics and the blood-stained altar, realizing that Carson was far more dangerous than she could ever have imagined.

"Riley," Carson's voice was traced with genuine panic, "I can explain."

"Explain?" she stammered, her wide eyes still fixed on the horrifying tableau before her. "How do you explain this?"

"It's, umm… It came with the house?" Carson said. "I have no idea what that is or how it got there?"

"That is the least convincing lie anyone has ever told me Carson," Riley spat, maybe made a little too bold by the whiskey.

"God damn it, I wanted to wait to do this," Carson sighed and took a step closer, his once-charming visage transformed into something monstrous and predatory. Shadows danced across his face, casting eerie patterns that seemed to bring out a darkness lurking within. "You've heard the stories," he said, his tone dripping with insinuation. "That vampires prey on the innocent at night, stalking the darkness. But we all know those are just children's tales and the invention of Hollywood."

"Are they?" Riley countered, her voice trembling as much as her legs. "Because this looks very real to me."

"Appearances can be deceiving," he replied with a sly smile that sent shivers down her spine. "But I assure you, there's nothing to be afraid of."

"Nothing to be afraid of?" Riley's mind raced, trying to reconcile the man she thought she knew with the monster standing before her. "That looks like a goddamn sacrificial altar, Carson!"

"It's not an altar to anything but progress," he conceded, shaking his head. "We are what comes next. It's just the next evolution of humankind."

"Is that what you're going with?" Riley responded, her incredulity overwhelming any sense of fear.

"I mean, it certainly sounded good in my head?" Carson shrugged. "I was planning on telling you about all of this, but it didn't really seem like a 'second date' sort of subject. Riley, I really like you. I hope this isn't a problem."

"You hope it isn't a problem that you're a vampire," Riley said, staring at Carson. "You hope the blood altar and being a vampire *isn't a problem? Are you being serious right now?!*"

Carson sighed, and sat down in a chair. "I mean, yes? When I say you're remarkable Riley, I genuinely mean that. You're brilliant, clever, and beautiful. Your understanding of complex political topics is unparalleled. I've never met anyone like you, and I was hoping you might eventually consider joining me."

"This is a lot, Carson?" Riley said, slowly backing towards the door.

"I want you to know that you've never been in any danger from me, Riley. All I want to do is give you a gift," Carson said, leaning forward on his knees. "I want you to accept it willingly, and help me bring this world into something new and glorious."

"God damn it, you're the Drake, aren't you," Riley asked quietly. "I meet someone attractive who seems to like me, and of course they turn out to be the god damn Drake."

Carson paused, "Yes I am… how do you know that name?" He rose to his feet, and stepped towards Riley.

"I think we've established I know lots of things," Riley said, trying to get to the door without taking her eyes off of Carson.

"I can't let you leave right now, Riley," Carson sighed, running his hand through his hair. "Not until I figure out what to do next. Please don't make me keep you here by force."

"I'm not staying here, Carson," Riley said, her eyes locked onto Carson's.

"Well I guess I'll just have to make you," he said, lunging towards her with a speed that defied human limits. His hand shot out like a striking viper, attempting to grab Riley by the shoulder.

Riley ducked and rolled, narrowly avoiding his grasp. Panic clawed at her insides, threatening to tear her apart as she scrambled to her feet. Carson was just behind her, moving with catlike grace.

"It's going to be okay Riley," he said, stalking her with a predator's grace. "In the end, we'll find a way to work this out. You'll see it my way."

Her heart hammered in her chest, each beat a desperate plea for survival. She searched her surroundings for any means of escape, knowing that time was running out.

Riley's fingers fumbled against the polished surface of a candlestick holder on Carson's mantelpiece. Her breath came in shallow gasps as her mind raced, calculating her next move. She glanced at the fireplace poker just out of reach, the cold iron offering a shred of hope.

"Come now, Riley," Carson called out, his voice oddly filled with sincerity. "Surely you can see the logic in this? You got your PhD at twenty-six. You're smarter than this. You could join me, and we could share in unimaginable power at the dawn of a new age of man."

"You do realize how insane that sounds!" Riley yelled back. She lunged for the poker and swung it with all her might, aiming for Carson's head. He dodged effortlessly, with almost a heartbroken look in his eyes. As he moved to seize her, Riley hurled the candlestick holder at him, forcing him to block the projectile. The brief distraction was enough, allowing her a moment to sprint out of the room. Carson was between her and the front door, so she needed a different exit.

"Running away?" Carson sneered. "You think you can escape destiny?"

"Watch me," she spat back, refusing to let fear control her. "I ran track in college."

Heart pounding in her ears, Riley bolted through the darkened townhouse, hoping desperately that the place had a back door. She needed to get somewhere Carson didn't expect. She couldn't go home.

"Riley, don't be foolish," Carson taunted, his voice echoing through the dimly lit hallway. "You know there's no getting away."

"Shut up!" she hissed, desperation lending her strength as she threw open the back door and stumbled onto the cold, wet pavement outside.

Adrenaline coursed through her veins, burning away the chilling tendrils of panic that threatened to immobilize her. The moonlit streets stretched before her like a labyrinth, but she knew which path led to salvation: Mia's apartment. She knew for a fact that Mia's home was cloaked from supernatural beings.

"Help me, Mia," she thought, praying that the connection they shared would give her friend some warning of the danger that pursued her. "Please..."

Riley's legs pumped furiously, her lungs aching with every ragged breath as she raced through the deserted streets. Fear clung to her, prickling along her spine as she imagined Carson's monstrous form giving chase.

"Almost there," she panted, ignoring the burning in her limbs as Mia's apartment building loomed into view. "Just a little farther..."

As she sprinted towards Mia's door, she could feel Carson's ominous presence bearing down on her, a dark cloud that threatened to swallow her whole. But Riley refused to give in.

Come and get me, you bastard, she thought fiercely, willing herself to run faster. *I'm not going down without a fight.*

Riley's trembling hand fumbled with the spare key she had been given a long time ago, her heart pounding in her ears as she finally managed to fit it into the lock. Swinging the door open, she stumbled into Mia's studio apartment, her breath ragged and gasping.

"Riley, what the hell–" Mia began, bolting upright in bed. Her voice caught in her throat as her eyes took in Riley's disheveled state, terror etched across her face.

"Carson... he's..." Riley panted, struggling to find the words as she clutched at her chest, trying to calm her racing heart.

"Bobbi," Mia barked, her tone sharp and urgent. "Get dressed and go. Now."

"Wha–" Bobbi stammered, confusion evident on her flushed face sitting up from under the sheets. But one look at Mia's grim expression was enough to silence her protests. Hastily grabbing her clothes, she slipped them on while glancing warily between Mia and Riley.

"Carson Smith. The Drake," Riley choked out, her voice barely more than a whisper. "Carson's the Drake, Mia. He attacked me..."

"Jesus Christ," Mia breathed, her eyes widening in horror. She swung her legs over the side of the bed and stood up, her own fear momentarily eclipsed by concern for her friend. "Are you hurt? Did he..."

"I don't think so," Riley shook her head, her vision swimming as she tried to make sense of the night's events. "I managed to get away, but I don't know if he followed me."

Mia crossed the room, her hands gripping Riley's shoulders as she looked her over with frantic intensity. "You did good, Riles. You got away. We'll figure this out, okay? We'll deal with this monster together."

"Thanks, Mia. I just... I didn't know where else to go," Riley breathed, her voice cracking with emotion.

"Hey, you came to the right place," Mia reassured her, her gaze softening. "You're always safe here."

Bobbi, now fully dressed, hesitated at the door, looking back at the two women. "Is there anything I can do?"

"Go back to your place, and maybe avoid the history department," Mia replied tersely, her eyes never leaving Riley's face. "It's too dangerous, Bobbi – and what I like about spending time with you is you *aren't* involved with this stuff."

"A little hard since I'm a history major and you just said the name of one of my profs," Bobbi muttered, swallowing hard. "But if some guy attacked your friend, remember I have a number of guns and I'm more than happy to use them."

"We don't need to shoot anyone, Bobbi," Mia said, shaking her head.

"Yeah, I was thinking 'threaten,' not injure, but if that's where your thinking is..." Bobbi shook her head. "You change your mind, you can always text or call me too. I know what we're doing here is just for fun, but part of being friends with benefits is, y'know, being *friends*."

Bobbi slipped out the door, casting one last glance over her shoulder as it clicked shut behind her and she disappeared into the night.

"Come on," Mia murmured, guiding Riley over to her bed and sitting her down. "Let's get you cleaned up, and then we'll figure out our next move. We've got a monster to deal with."

"Who'd've thought my pathetic love life would give us our biggest break," Riley said, managing a weak smile.

"It's definitely the worst kind of lucky," Mia said with a sigh.

Chapter 12

Mia climbed out of her old, rusty pickup truck and walked up to Lucy's house like a woman on a mission. She opened the door and walked into the living room without missing a beat.

"Riley managed to find the Drake," Mia announced confidently. She stopped and looked around the room, and realized it was empty.

"Where the hell is everyone?" Mia looked around. "Lucy? Sarah?"

"Lucy's upstairs with Jayla," a voice answered, as Emma walked into the room. The young vampire scrolled through her phone, only half looking up at Mia.

"Great, where's Sarah?" Mia replied.

"No idea. Haven't seen her all day," Emma shrugged. "But I didn't come out of the basement until a couple of hours ago, so I'm not sure when she left. I'm kind of out of the loop on most of this stuff."

Mia glanced around the room and located a small camera in the upper left corner of the room, and began to wave her arms, "Jayla! Have Lucy come down!"

"She's going to be a minute," Emma said, continuing to stare at her phone."When Lucy goes up there, she's usually feeding or fu–"

"I got it, I got it," Mia cut in, stopping Emma from completing the sentence. The two stood in silence for a minute, and Mia shifted awkwardly until the click of a hidden door echoed down the stairs.

"Emma? Get back in the basement!" yelled Lucy as she walked down the stairs.

"Literally no one I can eat is here!" Emma protested. "I can't bite the mall goth, remember?"

"Please," Lucy said quietly, entering the room and adjusting the strap on her black dress. Her hair was mildly disheveled, and Mia couldn't help but smirk to herself.

"Fine," Emma replied, rolling her eyes as she went through the hall door and retreated to the basement stairs.

"Okay, two things," Mia said, focusing on Lucy. "One, Riley found the Drake."

Lucy immediately perked up, her attention centered. "How?"

"She's been dating him, apparently?" Mia said, mildly bewildered.

"Riley, the small ordinary professor, has been *dating* the *Drake?*" Lucy said slowly, clearly taking a moment to process the information. "We've been been working this hard to find him, and the whole time she's been his paramour?"

"Like I think they've just gone out a couple of times and I don't think they've put a label on it, but *yes*," Mia explained. "She didn't know until tonight. She's currently hiding in my apartment because of it."

"Then we know where he is," Lucy nodded. "We should make a plan to move on him immediately."

"That's what I thought," Mia agreed. "But where's Sarah?"

"When dawn broke she went out to investigate the abandoned church you found last night," Lucy said thoughtfully. "I went to sleep upstairs around then, and only awoke a couple of hours ago. I had assumed she'd be back by now."

Mia felt a ball of anxiety forming in her stomach. "So she went out to where I found a pit of the Drake's vampires and never came back?"

Lucy nodded, realizing the implications of what Mia said. Mia pulled out her phone, flipping it open, but was immediately met with a low battery screen.

"Crap," Mia said shaking her head. "Okay, I have a charger in my truck, I'll try to call Sarah, and we're driving out to that church *now*."

****

Mia and Lucy pulled up to the abandoned church, now partly reduced to blackened timber and stone.

"She's still not answering," Lucy sighed, putting down Mia's phone as she stepped out of the truck.

Mia was already sprinting towards the ruins of the building, not wasting a moment. She began to scour the site, looking for any sign of Sarah. Half of the church was now collapsed, having suffered massive damage in the prior night's fire. It likely wasn't safe inside.

"Mia, over here!" Lucy called out

Lucy was pointing towards the ditch along the road, and Mia crossed the distance as fast as she could. Sitting about two hundred feet from the road was a deep green Subaru – Sarah's car. Mia slid into the ditch and began to examine the vehicle, with Lucy close behind.

"Doesn't appear to be any sign of struggle," Mia said, thinking out loud. "And I think I know why Sarah's not answering her phone." She picked up a cellphone from the center console of the car.

"There's no blood here," Lucy said, her brow furrowed. "I don't believe she's injured, but she may have been taken."

"God, why are we so *bad* at this?" Mia sighed, leaning against the car. "I almost die here escaping, my friend Nic *does* die, Sarah goes in to 'clean things up' and disappears, and the Drake has been under our noses the whole time."

"Luck doesn't seem to be on our side," Lucy said solemnly.

"We need to stop the Drake right now," Mia said, her voice as cold as steel. "If his people have Sarah, we need to save her. I'll text Riley and let her know what we're doing."

"Are you sure you're up to it?" Lucy asked. "You just recovered from your fight at the church."

"I'm not sure, but I don't think we have any other choice," Mia replied, her voice resolute. If Mia was being honest, she was really only at fifty percent, but she could feel the fire of determination burning within herself. "No one goes after my friends."

****

Mia parked her truck a block away from Carson's townhouse, and she and Lucy silently approached through the alley on foot, hoping to avoid attention. Light scattered from the kitchen windows through thick curtains as they made their way to the rear of the home. Sliding up to the back door, Mia pressed her ear to the thick wood and tried to listen.

"And why did you bring her *here*?" asked a deep voice. "That's the part I'm trying to figure out."

"She smells like the witch who burned down the church," replied a second person. "Sir, we thought you might want to question her!"

"I could have questioned her somewhere else, Jason," said the first voice, thick with irritation. "What if Riley had still been here? How would I have explained a woman tied to a chair to her? Where did you even *get* the chair?"

"I mean, not everything burned down at the church…"

"I can't deal with you right now, Jason," the first voice replied. "I need a drink and some time to think. I'll handle this later, keep her secured." The clear sound of a door slamming echoed in the night.

"At least one other person," Mia mouthed silently at Lucy. Lucy nodded in response.

She had to move now. They needed to get Sarah out. Mia quietly activated a series of sigils on her body, and she took a step back from the door. With a nod to Lucy, she kicked open the door, knocking the door clean off its hinges.

The four vampires in the kitchen looked incredibly surprised when a torrent of flame arced from Mia's hands, and Lucy and Mia charged in. Mia immediately spotted Sarah bound in the corner.

"Lucy, get Sarah free," Mia yelled, as she held off the four snarling and singed monsters.

Lucy ran over to Sarah and began to untie her bonds.

"I had things under control!" Sarah spat, as Lucy undid her gag.

"Yeah, it sure looks like it," Mia replied sarcastically.

"I found out who the Drake is finally!" Sarah yelled back, as she shrugged off the rest of her ropes.

"So did we!" Mia said, wielding another arc of flame at the vampires attacking her. "And we didn't get captured in the process!"

"We got lucky," Lucy admitted quietly.

"Lucky or not, we're here now," Sarah said, pulling a long silver dagger from its hiding place in her boot. "It's time to stop the Drake."

"Assuming we can figure out where the hell he went," Mia grunted.

The three women pushed deeper into the townhouse, and soon discovered Carson was far from alone tonight. Another dozen vampires greeted the trio in the living room.

The battle erupted in a frenzy of movement, a chaotic symphony of power and pain. Mia hurled a torrent of flame towards a group of vampires, the heat searing her skin and sending a thrill of adrenaline coursing through her veins. Lucy moved like mercury, flowing through the melee with grace and skill, avoiding the blows of her larger opponents while strategically striking where it could hurt the most, and Sarah brute forced her way through the crowd, the bodies of Carson's unsuspecting acolytes crumpling to the floor in a tangle of limbs.

Carson emerged from the shadows, his smirk an infuriating blend of arrogance and amusement. "Is this really all you've got?" he taunted, his voice dripping with condescension.

"Trust me," Mia snarled through gritted teeth, her blood boiling with rage. "You haven't seen anything yet."

In that moment, she felt a reckless abandon take hold, an unyielding need to destroy Carson. Maybe it was because he was a monster, or maybe it was just because he'd threatened Riley. Either way, he had to go, and Mia knew they would fight to the bitter end – until only one side remained standing.

Carson's eyes flashed with a predatory gleam, the air around him crackling with dark energy. "You think you can defeat me?" he hissed, a twisted grin stretching across his pale features. "You're just children playing at war."

Mia's heart pounded in her chest, her breath coming in ragged gasps as adrenaline surged through her veins. She locked eyes with Carson, refusing to be intimidated by an asshole in a suit. "We'll see about that," she spat, her fingers tracing intricate patterns in the air as she summoned as much power as she could muster.

"Ooh, looks like we've got a feisty one here," Carson said mockingly, gesturing towards Sarah. She glared up at him, her body tensed and ready for action.

"Feisty doesn't even begin to cover it," Sarah growled.

"Enough!" Lucy snapped, her voice cutting through the tension like a razor-sharp blade. The vampires that had been circling them hesitated, their crimson eyes flicking between her and Carson.

"Lucia Giamante Vitale? I almost didn't recognize you. My lord, I haven't seen you since Sicily in, what, 1849? Stay out of this, child," Carson snarled, his gaze never leaving Mia. "This is between me and these pathetic little humans."

Lucy's eyes narrowed dangerously, an icy chill creeping into her voice. "I will not stand idly by while you prey on the innocent. This ends now."

With supernatural speed, Lucy lunged forward, her powerful fists connecting with Carson's jaw before he could react. He stumbled back, caught off-guard by her ferocity, but quickly regaining his footing.

"Fine then," he sneered, wiping a trail of blood from the corner of his mouth. "It seems I do have an opening on my dance ticket."

As Carson launched himself at Lucy, his movements were a blur of speed and power, but Lucy met each strike with equal ferocity, her own supernatural strength allowing her to go toe-to-toe with the ancient vampire. Their battle was a dizzying whirlwind of violence, punctuated by the clash of flesh against flesh and the guttural roars of two predators locked in a deadly embrace.

Mia and Sarah fought the encircling vampires in an attempt to provide support and keep them our of Lucy's way. But every time they struck one down, two more seemed to take their place.

"Lucy!" she called out, her voice straining to be heard above the chaos. "I'm not doing great over here!"

"Keep your head in the fight, Mia," Lucy grunted, her face contorted with effort as she strained to keep her undead attackers at bay. "We can't afford any distractions."

"Easier said than done," Mia muttered, swallowing the lump in her throat. As she cast her next spell, a surge of electricity crackling from her fingertips,. The horde was unending, and she only recognized one or two of these vampires from her battle at the church.

How many more people had Carson turned?

As the scent of blood and sweat hung heavy in the air, Mia's senses were overwhelmed by the cacophony of battle. Her eyes darted from one face to another, registering their twisted expressions as they fought for their lives. The room seemed to shrink around her as her heart pounded in her chest, threatening to break free.

"Come on, you bastards," she hissed, her voice barely audible amidst the chaos. "You think you're so damn tough?"

Another vampire lunged at her, a snarl curling his lips. Mia narrowly dodged his claws, feeling the sharp edge graze her cheek. She retaliated with a swift kick to his gut, sending him crashing into the wall.

"Nice try," she smirked, her adrenaline surging. "But you'll have to do better than that."

"Hey, Mia!" Sarah called out, her voice strained. "I need a hand here!"

"Thought you'd never ask!" Mia yelled back, touching two of the sigil tattoos on the inside of her wrists together. A torrent of fiery magic shot towards the vampire pinning Sarah down, watching as he screamed in agony before collapsing to the floor.

"Thanks," Sarah gasped, wiping the sweat from her brow. "I owe you one."

"I owe you like a million already, so let's not keep count," Mia replied, a wry smile creeping onto her face.

Mia's resolve hardened, fueled by memories of her past struggles and the pain she had endured. She would not allow these monsters to continue terrorizing the town she now called home. She would fight, and she would protect those she cared about – no matter the cost. And if this was her last stand, at least she was here with Sarah. At least their story would end together.

Lucy's battle with Carson wasn't going well though, as the smaller vampire took a blow to the stomach, hard.

"No!" Mia screamed, as Lucy was thrown back, her body slamming against the wall with a sickening crunch.

"Lucy!" Sarah gasped. Mia and Sarah both rushed towards the injured vampire.

"Your time is up, witch," Carson sneered. "You and your pathetic allies have no chance against me."

"Go to hell," Mia replied, defiance blazing in her eyes even as despair threatened to swallow her whole.

"Perhaps," Carson mused, his gaze cold and unyielding. "But not before I send you there first."

Mia got to her feet, shaking as she tried to steady herself. Carson was moving towards the three of them now, and she had no intention of going down without a fight.

Just as Mia's resolve was about to be tested, the townhouse door exploded off its hinges with a deafening crash. Through the splintered remains strutted Bobbi, a large hunting rifle in hand.

Mia blinked in disbelief, her mouth practically hitting the floor. "Bobbi? What the actual hell?"

"I told you earlier, Mia. I have guns," Bobbi replied, a devilish grin spreading across her face. With a glint of determination in her eyes, Bobbi took a deep breath and aimed the hunting rifle at Carson. He stood there, smirking, his arrogance unwavering despite the sudden turn of events.

"Sweetheart, you don't have the guts," he taunted, his voice dripping with condescension.

"Watch me, shithead," Bobbi replied icily, her finger steady on the trigger. The air seemed to thicken around them as she squeezed, the gunshot echoing throughout the room like the crack of doom. The bullet found its mark, ripping through Carson's chest and sending him sprawling backwards, gasping in surprise.

Chapter 13

Riley sat alone in Mia's apartment, still shaken from her encounter with Carson early that night. The first guy she really liked in a long time turned out to be a murderous vampire.

How do you even begin to process that?

Her phone buzzed on the coffee table, jolting her from her thoughts. She picked it up and squinted at the screen. A text notification popped up from Mia: Carson had Sarah, and Mia and Lucy were going to try and get her back.

Riley's thoughts were a whirlwind of fear. Mia was barely recovered from the previous night, and Riley had seen first hand how dangerous Carson was. If Sarah was in trouble, Mia was going to charge in blind, and Riley needed to come up with a way to help.

"Damn it, Mia," she whispered, her heart pounding in her chest. "Why do you always have to bite off more than you can chew?"

As she paced the floor of the small studio apartment,, Riley's mind raced through her time with Mia. When an evil, vengeful spirit tried to get its hooks into Riley a year ago, Mia came along and put everything on the line to save her. Riley just didn't have anyone else in her life she could trust like Mia. The thought of losing her was unbearable.

"Alright, think, Riley, think," she muttered to herself, her eyes scanning the room for any hint of inspiration. Suddenly, a name popped into her head – Bobbi. Bobbi had been here when Riley first arrived, and said she'd be willing to help. Mia had repeatedly mentioned how much Bobbi liked hunting… like *normal* hunting.

Bobbi said she had guns.

"Bobbi… it's worth a shot." She picked up her phone and went to fire off a text, only to realize she didn't have Bobbi's number.

Shit.

Mia had to have it written down somewhere. Mia did everything manually. Any number she knew would have a hard copy for posterity.

Riley's heart pounded like it was going to burst out of her chest as she tore through Mia's apartment, her desperation palpable in the frenzied air. Papers flew like leaves in a hurricane, drawers slammed open and shut, and a fine layer of sweat coated her furrowed brow. The dim light from the apartment's single lamp barely gave Riley enough illumination to see a damned thing, heightening the sense of urgency that swirled around her.

"Damn it, where could it be?" Riley's voice trembled with frustration, a gnawing fear sinking its teeth into her gut. Her eyes darted from one corner of the room to another, searching for something – anything – that might connect her to Bobbi.

"Think, Riley, think!" She slammed her fist onto the wooden desk, the impact reverberating through her bones. "If I were Mia, a woman who refuses to use a smartphone, where would I keep the phone number of my regular hookup."

Riley went to Mia's desk that was shoved in the corner.

"Okay, okay…" Riley muttered to herself, her fingers dancing over the cluttered surface of the desk – old photos, crumpled receipts, half-empty cups of coffee gone cold. As she delved deeper into the chaos, her breath hitched, and time seemed to slow.

There it was: a crumpled piece of paper, hidden among the disarray like a secret waiting to be revealed. Trembling hands smoothed out the creases, revealing a name and the scrawled digits that held the key to their salvation.

"Gotcha," Riley whispered, her breath catching on the sharp edge of hope as she clutched the paper tightly in her hand.

Her thumb hovered over the screen of her phone, hesitating for just a moment before entering in the numbers. Each tap sounded like a ticking clock, counting down to an uncertain fate.

"Please please please be up," she pleaded. A shiver of adrenaline coursed through her veins as she started typing, fingers flying frantically over the screen. She willed herself to remain coherent, knowing that any confusion could spell disaster.

"Bobbi," she texted, "This is Mia's friend Riley. Mia's in danger. She went to go confront the guy who hurt me."

"Wait, what?!" Bobbi's response came faster than Riley could blink. "Why would she do that?"

"Carson's dangerous," she replied. "He tried to kill me, and he's killed others. He's not human."

"What do you mean 'not human?'" Bobbi sent back. "Is that a metaphor, or is that literal?"

"Literal. And you seem less shocked by this than expected," Riley quickly texted.

"Mia talks in her sleep, and sometimes I google what she says," Bobbi responded. "Way too much of it seems to be real."

"So yeah, Carson's a vampire," Riley said, in mild disbelief at how open to this Bobbi seemed to be. "He might have Sarah prisoner, and Mia went with our friend Lucy to save her. I need someone to help them."

The typing bubbles for Bobbi seemed to appear and disappear a few times before finally Bobbi responded.

"Sarah. Like SARAH Sarah?"

"Yeah. You seem more shocked by Sarah than Vampires?"

"Wouldn't you be at this point? Send me the address for Carson's. I'll get our girl out," Bobbi finally sent after a minute. Riley hastily sent Bobbi the address of Carson's townhouse.

She curled under the blanket of Mia's bed, hoping she'd done enough.

****

With the room still ringing from the gunshot, Bobbi didn't waste a moment. She stepped further into the fray, her rifle swinging left and right as she aimed for any vampire who dared approach her or the others.

"Let's go, you three," Bobbi snarled, her eyes flashing with urgency. "We don't have all night, and I'm just using my deer hunting ammo. You can't exactly buy silver bullets at Walmart."

Mia felt a surge of adrenaline course through her veins, fueled by the sudden appearance of their unlikely savior. She grabbed Sarah's hand and pulled her up to her feet. Lucy recovered more gracefully, rising in a single fluid motion that betrayed her supernatural nature.

"Alright, ladies," Mia said, panting heavily, "let's get the hell out of here before Carson grows a new lung."

As they raced toward the shattered front door, Bobbi led the way, pausing only to let off a few well-aimed shots at their pursuers. The sound of gunfire punctuated the air, mingling with the furious hisses of the remaining vampires.

Bobbi? Of all people, Bobbi saved us? Mia thought, her heart pounding in her chest like a drum. She couldn't believe how close they had come to meeting their demise, and now, against all odds, they were inching closer to freedom.

"Thank me later, get in the truck now!" Bobbi yelled, pointing them to the black F-150 parked on the street. They poured into the truck's crew cab, and Bobbi pushed the accelerator to the floor.

"Left!" Lucy shouted suddenly, directing them down an alleyway that connected to the main street. "My place is just a few blocks away. We'll be safe there. Carson doesn't know where I live."

"Sure hope so," Bobbi grumbled, barely braking as they turned the corner.

As they approached Lucy's house, the once imposing Victorian structure now seemed like a beacon of hope. The adrenaline from their escape began to fade, replaced by a mixture of exhaustion and gratitude. They gathered in the dimly lit living room, their hearts still pounding, their breath coming in ragged gasps.

"Safe at least for now," Lucy said, her voice barely audible. She glanced at the others, her eyes betraying a hint of vulnerability that belied her typically confident demeanor. "Thanks to this young woman."

"Bobbi, thanks to Bobbi," Mia said, collapsing on a couch.

"I told you I had guns, Mia," Bobbi replied, shaking her head. "Why the hell did you go into a fight like that without *guns.*"

Chapter 14

Mia, Sarah, Lucy and Bobbi sat in Lucy's living room, exhausted from the battle they had barely escaped. Mia almost jumped when the door creaked open.

She turned, and saw Riley walk through the door. Riley's tension seemed wash away, like a wave crashing on the shore. Her eyes darted around the room, settling on Mia.

"Thank God you're all okay," she breathed, moving quickly to embrace Mia. "Bobbi texted me you were fine, but I needed to see it for myself."

"Riley, we're all right," Mia reassured her, returning the hug. "It's been a rough twenty-four hours, but we're safe now."

"Rough is an understatement," Bobbi said, leaning back into her chair. "It's only hitting me now that I just shot the guy who teaches my Middle Eastern History class."

"Yeah, that probably won't help your grade," Riley smirked.

As the others shared a small laugh, Lucy slipped away, beckoning Sarah to follow her. They made their way upstairs, the muted sounds of conversation fading behind them as they entered Sarah's room. The flickering candlelight cast dancing shadows across the walls.

"Lucy," Sarah began coldly, "Carson recognized you. *The Drake* recognized you."

"It appears he did," Lucy said with a nod. She leaned against the edge of the dresser, moving with fluid grace.

"So you've met him before," Sarah said, a fire sparking in her eyes.

"Apparently? I genuinely have no memory of the man," Lucy said with a small shrug. "Most men I've met over the centuries have been wholly unremarkable. There are a few exceptions, but it seems the more important they think they are, the more forgettable they end up being."

Sarah stood taut like a pulled bow string, not sure if she should make a move or not.

"You're suspicious of me still, I understand," Lucy smiled, her voice almost like velvet. "There's a tension between us that I think we need to resolve."

"You're a vampire, I've spent a lot of the last year killing vampires," Sarah replied, her eyes locked on Lucy. "It doesn't seem too complicated to me."

"Sarah, we are more than our labels," Lucy whispered, closing the distance between them. "You are not just a hunter, and I am not just a vampire. We are both complex beings with desires and feelings. And I can see in your eyes that you're drawn to me more than you want to admit."

"You think you understand me," Sarah murmured. "The arrogance."

"Don't I?" Lucy asked. "Don't I understand what it's like to feel both human yet... not?"

Sarah shifted slightly. What Lucy was saying was true, but Sarah didn't want to admit it..

"You are a remarkable woman, one of the most remarkable women I've ever met," Lucy confessed, reaching out to brush a strand of hair from Sarah's face. "Even with half of your soul gone, you are still capable of feeling so deeply. It radiates from you, even when others think you're being cold."

Sarah turned, not quite able to maintain her eye contact with Lucy.

Lucy moved closer until she was standing directly behind Sarah, her breath tickling Sarah's ear like a cool breeze. She reached around Sarah to place her hand on her stomach, feeling the rise and fall of her breaths. Sarah shuddered at the touch, but didn't pull away.

"You don't have to fight your attraction to me," Lucy said, her voice low and seductive. "Just let yourself feel."

Sarah turned suddenly, grabbing Lucy by the shoulders and pushing her away. She stared at Lucy, eyes blazing with a mix of anger and desire.

"I can't do this," Sarah said, her voice trembling. "Not with something like you."

Lucy stepped back, looking hurt. "What do you mean 'something like me'?"

"Someone who preys on innocent people," Sarah spat. "Someone who's killed more people than I can even imagine. You may be beautiful and seductive, but that doesn't make you any less of a monster."

"I do not *prey on the innocent*," Lucy spat. "I have not fed from the unwilling in over a century, and the only deaths I may be responsible for were far from 'innocent.'"

"So you *have* killed," Sarah spat back.

"So have you," Lucy said quietly. "The vampires you killed tonight? They were people. Mostly college kids brainwashed after being turned against their will. Those were people with families and loved ones we fought. You dehumanize the things you hunt because it lets you sleep at night."

Sarah stood silently, not speaking.

"I found one of Carson's acolytes before he could 'save' her. You know this. You've seen Emma," Lucy said. "I'm doing what I can to train her so she can live her life normally without being a danger to others. What tore me up tonight was knowing I couldn't help or save our attackers. They were lost, and I had to make a choice."

Sarah's eyes searched Lucy's face, looking for any hint of insincerity, but there wasn't any to be found. The tension fled from her body as Sarah took a deep breath, processing everything Lucy had said.

"I'm sorry," Sarah said, her voice laced with regret. "I shouldn't have... I know you're not like the others."

"Actually, I'm quite typical," Lucy said softly, reaching out to touch Sarah's arm. "Most vampires know the only way to safely live around humans is to do so symbiotically. We feel guilt for the actions we take just like anyone else. We know what we do is wrong when we surrender to our hunger. Men like Carson are the exception, not the rule."

Sarah felt her anger dissipate, replaced by a strange mix of sadness and longing. Lucy was right; they were more than just their labels. She saw the pain in Lucy's eyes and knew that it wasn't just an act. Lucy was a complex being, just like she was.

"I want to believe you," Sarah said, her voice barely above a whisper. "But it's hard to ignore all the things I've seen."

"I understand," Lucy replied, her hand still resting on Sarah's arm. "But I'm not asking you to trust me blindly. I just want you to know that I'm not the monster you think I am. Anyone can be a monster or a saint. It's our choices that define us, not our circumstances."

Sarah looked into Lucy's eyes, feeling something stir deep within herself. For a moment the anger that she'd wrapped around herself like armor seemed to slip away.

Lucy leaned in, her lips hovering just inches from Sarah's. "Let me show you," she whispered.

Their lips met in a searing kiss, their bodies pressed against one another as if seeking solace from the darkness that surrounded them. Passion ignited between them like a wildfire, consuming them both in its relentless heat.

"Let me remind you what it means to be human," Lucy whispered into Sarah's ear, her breath now warm and inviting. She moved her lips down Sarah's neck, leaving a trail of burning kisses that made her shiver with pleasure.

"Lucy," Sarah gasped, her fingers tangled in the soft fabric of Lucy's dress. "This feels… oh hell, who cares.."

****

Jayla sighed as she stood up from the velvet plush couch and crossed the room to her monitors. She took one last look at Sarah and Lucy's passionate embrace before turning them off. Pulling her silk robe tight, she shook her head with a bemused smile.

The door creaked open, and Riley slipped into the room, casting a curious glance at the screens. "Couldn't help but notice Sarah slipping off with Lucy," she said. "Thought I'd come up for some fresh air and a healthy dose of voyeurism."

"Then come on in, the water's warm," Jayla said, walking back to the couch. "But I've turned the screens off. If you want to watch, you'll have to go downstairs and knock on the door."

Riley hesitated for a moment before settling down beside Jayla. "Wait, I was joking. I assumed they were having a conversation I could spy on."

"Oh no, they are doing very little talking," Jayla said smugly. "But I honestly don't know if Sarah realizes the cameras are there, so I'm choosing to give her privacy."

"And you're okay with that?" Riley paused for a second, continuing to watch. "I know you and Lucy are sort of a thing."

Jayla let out a soft chuckle. "I literally lock myself in her attic, and you're shocked that we're not monogamous? Polyamory's not even past most people's threshold of weird these days."

"I'm a simple woman I guess," Riley shrugged. "But hell, what ever works for you I guess?"

"What works for me right now is putting on old episodes of Star Trek and maybe making some popcorn," Jayla smiled. "Care to join me?"

****

Mia's fingers traced the intricate patterns of the protective sigil tattooed on her chest, each line a testament to her struggle against the demons that had once held her in their thrall. She shivered as she remembered the seductive allure of demonic possession, the insidious way it had wormed its way into her soul and left her craving more. It was a part of her that she would never completely put behind.

"Bobbi," Mia began, her voice barely above a whisper as she sat next to her on the worn couch in Lucy's living room. "There's something I need to tell you."

Bobbi looked at her curiously, her green eyes filled with concern. "What's up?"

"Remember how I told you I have a... complicated history with addiction?" Mia took a deep breath, gathering her courage. "It's way more complicated than I ever told you."

"Does it have to do with the fact that we just fought a bunch of vampires?" Bobbi responded. "Because vampires being real is a big deal to me still."

"There are worse things in the world than vampires, Bobbi," Mia sighed. "There are full fledged, purely evil, take over your body demons out there."

"Okay," Bobbi nodded quietly.

"I... what I was addicted to was demonic possession. Letting demons take over my body, to control me," Mia admitted quietly.

"Why would you do that?" Bobbi asked. "Why would anyone do that?"

"It's... it's an incredible high. I don't really have the words to describe it," Mia said shaking her head. "If it didn't feel incredible, no one would ever let themselves be possessed."

"Wow," Bobbi murmured, taking in Mia's confession with a mixture of awe and empathy. "I always imagined the day you'd actually tell me something real about yourself would come."

"You're not as shocked as I thought you'd be," Mia said, shifting nervously.

"I've seen some of the books you leave lying around your apartment – the ones about magic and monsters," Bobbi explained. "And you talk about it in your sleep sometimes, too. I started looking up some of the words I didn't recognize, and stuff started becoming pretty clear a while ago."

Mia blushed, suddenly feeling exposed. "It did?"

Bobbi nodded, her expression softening. "Yeah. But don't worry, your secrets are safe with me."

"Thanks," Mia whispered, grateful for Bobbi's understanding. "When a demon takes over you, it supplants your power, and your will..."

"Are vampires a kind of demon?" asked Bobbi, leaning back on the couch.

"Not quite?" Mia explained. "Vampires are related to demons, their power comes from a similar possession. But while the spirit that causes vampirism holds on like a vice, it can't control a person. It just drives up your desires and hunger instead of actually subverting your will. So like if a demon possessed a..."

Mia trailed off, lost in thought for a moment.

"Oh fuck, I think I have an actual idea."

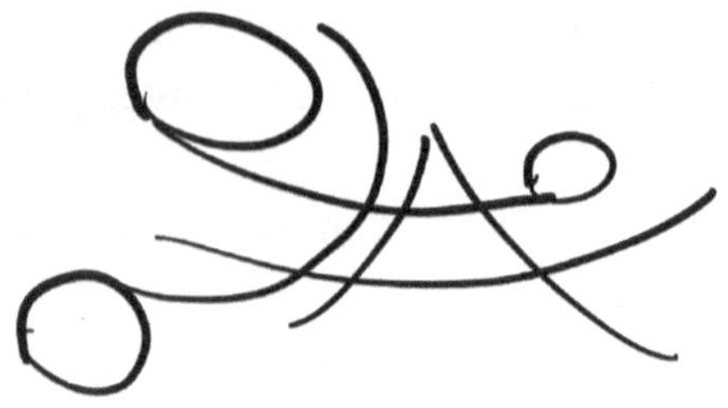

Chapter 15

Under the dim light of a chandelier overhead, Mia stood in the center of Lucy's living room, her eyes scanning the faces gathered around her. Lucy, Bobbi, Riley and Sarah all looked up at her with varying expressions of curiosity and concern.

"Alright, everyone," Mia began, clearing her throat and clasping her hands together. "We need to talk about how we're going to deal with Carson. And I think I've figured out a plan."

"Hope it's better than your 'run in and get killed' plan," Riley said, leaning back in a high backed chair. "Because that was a bad plan."

"We underestimated him," Lucy sighed, shifting on the velvet couch. "We won't make that mistake again. What is your plan, Mia."

"Everything comes down to how vampires actually *work*," Mia said, her voice steady despite the butterflies fluttering wildly in her stomach, "if you didn't know, vampirism is caused by the possession of a 'vampiric spirit.' These spirits aren't quite the same as demons." She glanced at Sarah, their eyes locking for a moment, a shared understanding passing between them. "They don't subjugate the will of the people they possess, but the possession operates on the same principles."

"Why does everything come down to possession with you guys," Riley muttered quietly to herself, her brow furrowed as she swirled the whiskey in her glass.

"There's another important difference between vampires and demons," Mia continued. "Unlike most demons, these spirits are almost impossible to exorcize. That's why you can't easily cure a vampire."

"So we can't un-vampire Carson," Sarah said, her voice barely a whisper, "I don't think that's really news."

"I'm not done," Mia said, taking a deep breath and feeling the weight of their gazes on her. "As you know, Sarah, two things can't possess a person at the same time. You sort of... hit capacity."

"How does that help us," Riley asked.

"If someone were to summon a powerful demon into, say, a vampire... the demon and vampire would have to fight to stay there," Mia said with a smirk. "All of their energy would be bound into their own survival, and not available to the person they're possessing. The person would become temporarily mortal."

"That would make killing him a hell of a lot easier," Riley said, leaning forward.

"Sounds convenient." Sarah crossed her arms over her chest, her eyes narrowed in thought.

"Do you remember what happened to Charlie in that old garage three years ago?" Mia asked quietly, a dark memory bubbling to the surface.

"Yeah. You're saying that's why he..." Sarah said, her eyes opening wide. "Fuck, I don't think I've ever put that together."

"Nothing's ever certain when it comes to the supernatural," Mia admitted, feeling the familiar tug of doubt deep within her. She shook it off as quickly as she could. "However, we've seen it happen before, and I think it's our best shot."

The room sat silent for a moment. Mia looked at her friends, trying to get a gauge of their reactions. Lucy, who had been listening intently, seemed deep in thought as she considered Mia's words. Riley looked conflicted, and Sarah remained as stone faced as ever. Eventually Mia's eyes fell on Bobbi. She was absorbing all of this like a sponge. A pang of guilt hit Mia's stomach when she thought about how this ordinary girl had been dragged into her world.

"Okay, so if we want to try this," Riley finally asked, "how do we go about summoning a demon into Carson?"

"Carefully," Mia answered in a measured tone. She took a deep breath, and locked eyes with her friends. "I'll need to be the one to do it. I'll perform a ritual to summon a demon powerful enough to challenge the vampiric spirit within him. If everything goes as planned, they'll clash, temporarily rendering Carson mortal."

"Mia," Sarah said quietly. "Are you okay doing this."

"I'm not directing it into me, Sarah," Mia replied. "I'm directing it into Carson. And yeah, it's dangerous."

"Then what?" Sarah's voice was tense. "We just waltz in and kill him while he's vulnerable?"

"Essentially, yes," Mia replied, trying to ignore the knot of fear tightening in her stomach.

"And what happens if we don't kill him and the demon wins the fight?" Riley asked. "Won't we have a demon on our hands then?"

"Vampiric spirits aren't strong, but they're almost impossible to kill. I don't think I'm powerful enough to even summon a demon strong enough to *hurt* one," Mia said shaking her head.

"We are the cockroaches of the supernatural world," Lucy chimed in. "Easy to step on, but impossible to get rid of."

"Look, it won't be easy, but I believe we can do it." Mia said, hoping she sounded strong enough to inspire confidence.

"I'm still concerned about the very idea of you working with demons," Sarah said, her eyes narrowing with suspicion. "How do we know that in the heat of the ritual you won't be tempted to draw the demon into yourself instead of Carson?"

"That's valid, and I'm worried about that too." Mia said quietly. "That's where Bobbi, Riley, and Lucy come in."

Bobbi straightened, remembering she was an active participant in the room.

"You three will stay with me as I cast the spell," Mia continued, her voice firm with determination. "You'll make sure I'm not tempted, and stop me if I start to redirect the demon into myself."

"Fine," Sarah conceded, her gaze never leaving Mia's. "But that leaves me alone to kill Carson. You're putting a lot on just me with a silver blade."

"True," Mia admitted, her heart pounding with anticipation. "But we'll make sure he's alone when you confront him, and since he'll temporarily be mortal, you should have no problem killing him."

"Wait, why don't we just shoot Carson? Once he's human, you could just shoot him in the head," Bobbi blurted out.

Blank stares from the rest of the women greeted her question like raindrops on a still pond.

"Why are you all acting like that was a stupid question?" Bobbi asked, blinking.

"It's not, it's just... guns complicate things," Mia sighed, rubbing her temples. "This will be close quarters, and there's every chance he might disarm Sarah at some point. Human Carson with a gun ruins everyone's day."

"Besides," Lucy added, her silken voice exuding an air of experience, "a more... direct approach ensures that his demise is certain. Decapitation is likely our only sure bet."

"Alright, then." Sarah stood up, her muscular form radiating both fear and excitement. "When are we doing this."

"Tomorrow night. I think we all need to rest before we go on the attack," Mia said. "I definitely need to recharge before I'm throwing any powerful spells around."

As the group dispersed to make their final preparations, Mia found herself deeply conflicted. It was the best plan, it really was – but it meant she had to touch a darkness which had once slithered under her skin and whispered her sweet lies. Her sigils meant whatever demon she summoned couldn't force its way in, but they wouldn't stop her from opening the door herself. Was she really going to be able to get this close and not give in to temptation?

"Hey," Riley murmured, placing a hand on Mia's shoulder. "Whatever happens, we've got your back."

"Thanks," Mia whispered, the warmth of Riley's touch anchoring her to the present. "I won't let you down."

Mia really hoped that was true.

****

As Sarah approached Carson's townhouse, the moon cast an unearthly glow upon the building, painting it in shades of pale blue and black. Sarah pressed her back against the cold brick wall, feeling the rough texture beneath her fingertips as she peered around the corner to assess the situation. She could see Carson sitting in the living room alone, with no sign of movement from any of the other windows. Sarah circled around to the rear of the block, making her way to the opposite side of the row of houses. No movement came from any of the windows of Carson's home here either.

"Looks like he's all alone," she quickly typed into her phone. "No sign of backup or visitors."

"Good," came Mia's reply, the bubble popping up on Sarah's screen. "We'll begin the ritual now. Stay on high alert and wait for our signal."

"Understood," Sarah responded, her heart pounding like a drum against her ribcage. As she crouched in the shadows, watching Carson's townhouse with hawk-like focus, Sarah couldn't help but feel a sense of dread creep over her. This was it – the moment they had been planning for.

"Stay strong," she murmured to herself, the words wrapping around her like a protective charm. "You can do this."

****

Mia stood in the dimly lit living room, surrounded by flickering candles casting ghostly shadows across the walls. The scent of burning herbs and incense filled the air, creating a heady atmosphere that sent shivers down her spine. She glanced around at Lucy, Riley, and Bobbi, their expressions holding varying degrees of concern. She knew they had faith in her.

Mia just wished that she did too.

"Alright, here goes nothing," Mia muttered, her fingers tracing the intricate protective sigils she had drawn on the floor. She could feel the power thrumming within the

153

symbols, tingling against her skin like a live wire. "You all know what to do. Keep me grounded, and don't let me waver."

"Trust us," Riley said, her voice unwavering. "We won't let you down."

Mia began chanting the necessary incantations, her voice low and hypnotic. She could feel the power building within her, a maelstrom of dark energy pulsing through her veins like an electric current. Bobbi, Riley, and Lucy silently exchanged glances.

Mia's eyes locked onto the protective symbols as she continued to chant. The air around them crackled with energy, the very atmosphere alive with anticipation.

"Carson won't know what hit him," Bobbi whispered, her eyes gleaming with excitement.

Let's hope not, Mia thought, her heart pounding as she pushed herself to the limits of her ability, knowing that Sarah's survival – and their collective future – hung in the balance.

One of the unlit candles surrounding Mia flickered to life on its own, soon followed by a second one. One by one, each sparked to a flame, lit by the ambient magic. She winced as she pricked the tip of her finger, allowing bright red droplets to fall onto the sigils she had drawn on the floor. The scent of herbs and wax mixed with the metallic tang of blood in the air.

"Damn, that stings more than I remembered," Mia muttered, trying to mask her unease. She glanced at her friends, their faces illuminated by the dancing flames. "Some kinds of penetration are less fun than others."

"Mia, not the time," Lucy replied, her worry evident. "Very much not the time."

"I know, I know." Mia took a deep breath, her mind racing with thoughts of Sarah, Carson, and the demon she was about to summon. This was it – the culmination of all their planning and preparation, the moment when everything could go wrong.

As the words flowed from her lips, Mia felt the familiar pull of dark energy, the seductive allure of demonic power. It would be so easy to let it flow into her instead of Carson, to indulge in the intoxicating thrill of possession once more.

"Hey, dipshit!" Riley's voice pierced through Mia's thoughts like an arrow, breaking her concentration. "I know that face. That's your bad idea face. Remember what we talked about. This isn't for you."

"Fuck, sorry, sorry," Mia whispered, her eyes filling with gratitude. "Just a passing thought, I'm still in control."

"Damn straight you are," Bobbi chimed in, flashing a determined smile. "Just keep it that way."

****

Sarah moved confidently towards Carson's back door, feeling both invigorated and terrified. Her pulse raced, adrenaline coursing through her veins like liquid fire. With each step, memories of her tumultuous past with Mia and their shared addiction to demonic possession washed over her – the pain, the ecstasy, and the darkness that threatened to swallow them whole.

Her concern for Mia's safety kept creeping to the front of her mind.

"Focus," Sarah whispered to herself, shaking off the weight of those memories. "You've got one shot at this."

She took a deep breath, savoring the crisp night air as it filled her lungs, then pulled a lockpicking kit from her pocket. There was no turning back. A wicked smile tugged at the corners of her lips as she thought of Carson's imminent demise.

After a few moments, and with a few satisfying clicks, Sarah rotated the cylinder and unlocked the door.

Opening the door slowly, she stepped over the threshold of Carson's townhouse. The air was thick with anticipation, and Sarah moved with absolute silence. As she ventured further into the dimly lit space, her instincts screamed at her to be ready for a fight to the death.

"Carson, you smug bastard," she muttered under her breath, gripping her weapon tightly as she scanned the shadows. "It's time to put an end to your little game."

"Ah, the little hunter." Carson's voice slithered out from the darkness, sending shivers down her spine. "I thought you'd come back eventually."

"Of course you did." Sarah rolled her eyes, her fear momentarily overridden by annoyance. "You really do fancy yourself a mastermind, duck-boy."

"What?" Carson paused, confused.

"You call yourself 'the Drake,'" Sarah said. "You know, like a male duck."

"It's… it's not Drake as in *duck*, it's Drake as in *Dragon*," Carson replied with an annoyed tone.

"If you wanted to be called dragon, you should have gone with that instead of the one that means duck," Sarah shrugged.

"It wasn't even originally in English," Carson said, his figure slowly emerging from the gloom. "They have completely different etymologies."

"I really don't care," Sarah replied, her voice cold and hard as steel. "It's poor branding either way."

****

Mia steadied herself, resisting the temptation of demonic power coursing through her. Her heart raced, sweat beading on her forehead as she channeled the dark energy toward Carson, hoping that her insane plan would work.

"Here goes nothing," she whispered, her voice barely audible over the pounding of her own heart.

Mia's throat tightened as she began to chant the final incantation of the spell, her voice growing steadier with each word. The room buzzed with a palpable energy, the air crackling like an electric charge. Focusing intently on Carson, Mia imagined the demon X'Hwyrth'il clawing its way toward him, ready to wrest control from the vampiric spirit that was buried inside him.

"X'Hwyrth'il, ignoth th'lin'tar," she whispered, her voice carrying an uncanny power. She could feel the demon's presence, its hunger for chaos and destruction gnawing at the edges of her consciousness. It took every ounce of her willpower not to succumb to its allure.

"Stay the course, Mia," Riley urged, her hand gripping Mia's shoulder. "Keep it steady."

Riley's hand felt like a guiding rudder, a reassuring guidepost keeping her on track. With a sense of purpose, she continued the incantation, her voice rising in volume and intensity.

"X'Hwyrth'il, ignoth v'rth'iz'na!" she cried out, sending a wave of energy coursing through the room. Mia could feel the demon's energy surging around her, her entire being vibrating with its essence. It was just dancing on the edge of her mind, and Mia knew that touching it for herself and letting it enter her was just a hair away. It would be so easy to just let it fill her right now. To let the waves of pleasure crash into her and surrender her being.

But that wouldn't keep Sarah safe or stop Carson's plan. Mia was not about to give in. Mia would never do anything to risk Sarah again.

Her voice reached a crescendo, the final words of the incantation spilling from her lips like a tidal wave.

"X'Hwyrth'il, ignoth k'ran'ak'no Carson Smith!"

With the last syllable, the energy in the room exploded outward, invisible tendrils seeking their target.

"May X'Hwyrth'il find you, you piece of shit," Mia muttered under her breath, feeling a cold satisfaction wash over her.

****

Sarah stared down Carson with steely eyes, her entire body coiled like a spring, ready to strike. As her adversary lunged toward her, his fangs bared and his nails elongated into razor-sharp claws, she nimbly sidestepped his attack, delivering a swift kick to his abdomen.

"Is that all you've got?" she taunted, her lips curling into a confident smirk. "I expected more from someone with your reputation. Where's the big bad I fought the other night?"

"Careful what you wish for, my dear," Carson hissed, launching himself at her again. "I'm just playing with my dinner. It's no fun if I don't let you put up a fight."

Sarah dodged his advances with cat-like reflexes, her senses heightened by both adrenaline and the knowledge that Mia's spell could make or break their mission. She was one with the moment, her body moving without conscious thought. She was instinct, she was the movement itself.

Sarah's senses picked up on the sudden shift in the atmosphere. The air crackled with an otherworldly presence; she could almost taste its familiar malevolence on her tongue.

It tasted like honey.

A darkness seemed to flow around Carson. He faltered mid-attack, his body spasming violently as the demon entered him.

"Wha... what have you done?" he snarled, his voice strained by the internal battle raging within him.

"Let's just say we've leveled the playing field," Sarah replied, smirking. "Meet X'Hwyrth'il, your new temporary roommate."

Carson's eyes flashed with a mixture of rage and fear, the two entities warring for control over his body. The veins bulged beneath his sweat-drenched skin, his face a mangled canvas of agony and rage. The stench of sulfur filled the room, seeping into Sarah's nostrils with every labored breath she took.

"Looks like you're having a bit of a possession problem," Sarah taunted, her voice dripping with schadenfreude despite the very real fear gnawing at the edges of her resolve. She tightened her grip on the silver dagger in her hand, its cold metal biting into her palm. "Don't worry, though. I'm here to help."

"Damn you," Carson spat through gritted teeth, his words barely intelligible as his body heaved with the force of the supernatural battle raging within him. His eyes flickered between their normal icy blue and a hellish, glowing red – a chilling reminder of the demon X'Hwyrth'il trying to assert control over him.

"Actually, I think it's more about damning *you* right now," Sarah retorted, her lips curling into a sinister smile that didn't quite reach her eyes. A shudder of revulsion rippled through her as she watched the gruesome spectacle before her, but she knew she couldn't afford to hesitate any longer.

With a surge of adrenaline-fueled determination, Sarah lunged forward, her long, silver dagger slicing through the air like a vengeful avenging angel. Carson's eyes widened, but he was powerless to react as the blade slashed across his neck.

His head made a sickening thud as it hit the floorboards of the townhouse.

"I'd say something witty here, but no one's around to hear it," she whispered, her voice laced with satisfaction and sadness. The final moments of a hunt were always bittersweet.

His body hadn't dropped to the ground yet, still held upright by the swirling dark energy that seemed to be now whipping around it like snakes of smoke. The air was heavy with the oppressive weight of that dark energy, as his headless body began to shake.

And then, all at once, it was over.

Carson's lifeless body crumpled to the floor. Shadowy tendrils of smoke rose from his corpse, wrapping around him like a lover's embrace as they consumed him in hellfire. Within moments, there was nothing left but ash and the lingering stench of sulfur, a grim testament to the man he had been and the monster he had become.

For a heartbeat, Sarah stood there, staring at the charred pile of ash that had once been Carson Smith. A wave of emotions crashed through her – relief, sorrow, anger, and exhaustion – leaving her breathless and spent.

"Time to go," she muttered under her breath, pulse thrumming in her ears. She knew she didn't have long before someone would come to investigate the commotion, and the last thing she needed was to be caught red-handed – both literally and figuratively.

Sarah hurried across the room, carried forward largely by momentum. The fight had taken more out of her than she'd realized, and her breathing came in ragged gasps. As she approached the door, she paused for a moment, allowing herself one final glance back at the grisly tableau she was leaving behind.

"Sorry for the mess," she said with a bitter smile.

With that, she slipped out the back of Carson's townhouse, and made her way back to Lucy's.

Chapter 16

Mia sank into the plush velvet cushions of Lucy's antique chaise longue, the soothing aroma of cinnamon and clove incense wafting around her. The flickering flames of candles cast dancing shadows across the dimly lit living room, wrapping the space in an almost cozy warmth. She absentmindedly traced the intricate rune and sigil tattoos etched onto her forearm, the familiar sensation like a balm against her frayed nerves.

"Carson was the head of the snake, but he's not the end of the threat," Riley said, pulling Mia back into the conversation. Her voice carried an edge of anxiety that grated against the room's tranquil ambiance. "All those newly turned vampires are still out there, and who knows what they're capable of?"

"Or who will end up controlling them," Sarah added, her tone dark as she sipped from a glass of red wine. Her gaze lingered on Mia for a moment too long, causing a shiver of unease to skitter down Mia's spine. "Job ain't done."

Mia rolled her eyes internally, already exhausted by their collective paranoia. "I get that we're still kind of fucked, but let's not forget we *won*. Can't we enjoy that for a whole minute?" Her exasperation hung heavy in the air.

"Perhaps we should focus on finding a way to restore order instead of indulging in melodrama," Lucy said quietly. She lounged gracefully in an armchair, her porcelain skin glowing against the ruby fabric. "These people are lost, and there's a chance we can help bring them around."

Riley sighed, running a hand through her disheveled blonde hair. "You're right. But first, I'm going to go to check on Jayla. Everyone forgets about Jayla." Pushing herself out of her chair, Riley stood and made her way to the door.

"I didn't forget about Jayla. I never forget about Jayla," Lucy said quietly. "I literally was up there an hour ago."

"I didn't think anyone forgot about Jayla," Sarah said. "Little red light comes on on the cameras when she's looking at you or what you're doing."

"Who's Jayla?" asked Bobbi, looking slightly confused.

The creaking of old wooden stairs accompanied Riley's ascent, the sound echoing in her ears as she navigated the dimly lit passageway. She paused outside Jayla's door, hesitating for a moment before undoing the latches to the secret entrance to the attic, and locked the door behind her.

"Hey Riley," Jayla's melodic voice beckoned from within.

Riley stepped inside the small attic apartment, and spotted Jayla's vulnerable form sitting on the edge of an antique bed. She seemed almost fragile in the dim light.

"Hey," Riley murmured, crossing the room to sit beside her. "How are you holding up?"

Jayla offered a weak smile. "I'm good," she whispered, her fingers dancing nervously on her lap. "Sorry if I'm a little weak right now, I let Lucy feed off of me an hour ago, and it always leaves me a little wobbly."

"I can tell," Riley said, placing a comforting hand on Jayla's shoulder. "Yikes, you look like you've been run over by a bus."

"Yeah, but it's so worth it," Jayla breathed, her voice trembling ever so slightly. "You have no idea how good it feels."

"It better if it leaves you like this," Riley replied, looking at the fragile young woman before her. "Can I get you anything?"

"No... want to spy on your friends up here?" Jayla smiled, gesturing towards the array of monitors.

"Oh hell yes," Riley smiled. "I want popcorn, do you have popcorn?"

"There's some microwavable packs in the cabinet," Jayla laughed.

"Y'know, for a post victory gathering, there's been very little makings out between those four," Riley sighed, walking to the small kitchenette on the far side of the attic. "It's very unlike this crowd. I've seen Mia celebrate getting a *tax return*."

"Just wait," Jayla laughed. "Someone's going to boil over soon, just you wait."

****

The shadows stretched long and sinuous across the hardwood floors of Lucy's living room, as Sarah watched Riley go upstairs. Everyone's nerves were at their frayed edge.

"Bobbi," Sarah murmured, her dark eyes flicking to the younger woman, who lounged in an overstuffed armchair. "Can I talk to you for a second?"

"Sure thing, scary lady," Bobbi replied with a grin, pushing herself up and sauntering over to Sarah, whose heart clenched at the sight of her carefree demeanor. She knew the risks that came with this life – knew the darkness that lurked just beneath the surface of their world – and she'd be damned if she let anything happen to the impulsive college girl.

"Listen," Sarah began, her voice low and urgent as she led Bobbi into the dimly lit hallway. "I appreciate everything you've done, but I don't think you understand what you're getting yourself into here. This isn't some kind of supernatural joyride. People get hurt, or worse."

Bobbi rolled her eyes and crossed her arms over her chest. "Cut the crap, Sarah. That danger? It was out there before I knew about it. I wasn't any safer not knowing about it."

"Is that right?" Sarah challenged, her gaze unwavering. "Then tell me, have you ever looked into the eyes of a vampire as they tear into your flesh? Felt the icy grip of death clawing at your throat?"

Bobbi sighed. "No, but I've been the one queer girl in a small town, and have met plenty of folks who thought they could 'fix' me, whether I consented or not."

Sarah stood there for a moment, not really having a response. "I don't think you realize that as you go into this world, Mia won't always be there to save you."

A flicker of doubt passed over Bobbi's face, but she quickly masked it with a defiant smirk. "Since *I'm* the one who saved *Mia* the other day, I don't think that's too much of a shock," Bobbi shook her head. "And Mia wasn't ever going to save me. Hell, she barely even likes me a lot of the time."

"Bobbi," Sarah sighed, feeling a pang of empathy for the brash young woman. "Mia is... complicated. She's been through a lot, and I know she can be frustratingly guarded at times."

"Try infuriatingly closed off," Bobbi corrected, frustration tinting her voice. "But you're her ex, so you should know all about that, right?"

"Maybe," Sarah admitted, her mind flickering back to the countless late-night conversations and heated arguments they'd shared. The memory of Mia's evasive gaze stung like a fresh wound. "But beneath all of that sarcasm and those walls she's built, there's a vulnerable soul who's just trying to protect herself. She was… she was on her own starting at fifteen. The walls are there for a reason."

"Maybe," Bobbi muttered, her eyes filled with irritation. "But at this point I don't know if it's worth trying to break through. She's fun for a night here and there, but she doesn't seem to actually like me enough for anything more."

Sarah stood there silently, absorbing what Bobbi had said.

"I'm here because the whole town was in danger. I'm here because Mia needed me," Bobbi said. "But you don't have to try and convince me that I can't count on her or that no one will come to save me. That was my life already."

****

The scent of damp earth hung in the air as Mia descended the creaky wooden stairs into Lucy's dimly lit basement. Her footsteps echoed through the cavernous space.

"Emma?" Mia called out, her voice softer than she intended. She spotted the young vampire at the far end of the room, her short, artificially red hair reflecting what little light was there while she focused intently on a flickering candle flame. A small cat ran past Mia's legs and ran up the stairs.

"That cat's been down here for three hours," Emma said quietly. "It's the first one that's made it that long. Didn't even try to eat it."

"Damn, that's impressive," Mia admitted, allowing herself a small smile. "You're getting better at controlling your hunger."

"Thanks," Emma replied, her voice laced with pride and something else Mia couldn't quite place. "Lucy's been helping me. She says it's crucial for me to find balance. Honestly I just want to feel like I can trust myself going outside again."

It wasn't lost on Mia how much importance Lucy placed on control, especially after witnessing the devastating effects of losing it. As they locked eyes, Mia felt a strange sense of kinship with Emma, two souls teetering on the edge of chaos, struggling to keep the darkness at bay.

"I just wanted to see how you were doing," Mia said softly, placing a reassuring hand on Emma's shoulder. "I'm glad you're improving."

"Lucy says I *might* be able to go outside soon... supervised of course," Emma sighed. "And at night. She thinks I'd make it a good hour in the sun right now, but neither of us is anxious to test that bit."

"That's... wow," Mia blinked a few times. "I'm impressed?"

"Don't be," Emma sighed. "It's actually not that hard to resist the sun, someone just has to bother teaching you how."

"The man who turned you, he didn't seem to care about it," Mia sighed. "I'm glad he can't turn anyone else ever again."

"Yeah, that's good," Emma said. "I'm glad Lucy found me. Now... if you could go. It's incredibly hard to keep my focus on this candle while I can hear your heart beat this closely."

Mia nodded and silently climbed back up the stairs.

"Hey, Mia," Lucy called from the doorway of a small parlor off of the main hall, her voice as smooth and inviting as a glass of aged bourbon. "Care to join me for a moment?"

"Sure," Mia replied, feeling a familiar warmth stir within her as she entered the dimly lit room. The scent of lavender and candle wax hung heavy in the air, reminding her of one evening she spent tangled in Lucy's sheets months ago.

"Sit down," Lucy whispered, gesturing toward the plush, velvet-covered sofa. As Mia sank into the cushions, she couldn't help but wonder if this was just another fleeting moment of intimacy, destined to be snuffed out like a candle flame when the darkness threatened to consume them once more.

"So, the legion of discount vampires the Drake left behind, what's your plan to deal with them," Mia sighed, feeling the velvet of the cushion between her fingers.

"The only way I know how," Lucy sighed. "Give them the choice I gave Emma when I found her and try to teach the willing ones. The rest... I have no idea."

"It's weighing a lot on you," Mia said quietly.

"You know what that's like from what I can tell," Lucy smiled. "What you risked for all of us... I don't know if anyone but Sarah knows how dangerously close you must have been to surrendering."

"Understatement of the century," Mia laughed. "It took every last bit of willpower I had."

"You've been through a lot," Lucy sat down next to her on the chaise, her hand brushing Mia's knee. "You really are a remarkable woman, Mia Graves. I just don't know if you realize it."

Mia blinked for a moment, taking note of how close Lucy was. How Lucy's hand lingered by her thigh. How Lucy had closed the door behind them. "So, uh, what's happening here?"

Lucy stopped moving, "What do you mean?"

"I mean, you're doing that seductive creature of the night thing," Mia said, furrowing her brow. "Like you did this with Sarah the other night. We did this months ago when we first met. You sidle up to someone, move in all fluidly and graceful, tell them how amazing they are, then sleep with them. I'm not saying it's a bad thing, but it's clearly, like, your go to *play*."

"I... I just..." Lucy stuttered for a moment. "It's not a 'creature of the night' thing, I move like this. It's literally just how I move. I moved like this *before* I was a vampire."

"Doesn't explain the rest," Mia smirked.

"Okay, so I like having sex with people," Lucy said, mildly bewildered. "That is a normal thing. Hell, you've slept with almost everyone in this house. Your ex and your current-whatever are at this moment having a heated conversation about you right now down the hall."

"I'm not... I'm not judging the sex part. You're very good at sex, you get consent, and I doubt anyone's ever complained," Mia said shaking her head. "It's more so your whole super-seductive 'oh you're so special, let me make you feel special' schtick that goes with it."

"It's not 'schtick' if the person I say it to actually *is* special," Lucy replied quietly. Her composure faltered for a moment, "A group of attractive, remarkable women in a high stress scenario came into my house, of course I'm going to ask if they want to have sex with me during the few moments of quiet. I'm not an idiot."

"It's just... it's just weird," Mia said. "Red flags all around."

"Really. Red flags," Lucy said crossing her arms. "My saying 'I find you very attractive' is a 'red flag?' You do understand how ridiculous that sounds, right?"

"I just feel like you're using your sexuality in manipulative ways," Mia said, sliding away. "Like your primary way of dealing with people is through your sexuality."

Lucy sat there for a minute. "Mia, I'm saying this with love and grace, but you need to listen to what you just said and look in a mirror."

Silence hung in the air for a while. Mia tried to avoid making eye contact with Lucy for as long as possible.

"So, I made this weird, huh," Mia sighed.

"Only a little," Lucy replied, patting Mia on the shoulder. "On the upside I very much do *not* want to have sex with you anymore. At least not tonight."

****

Bobbi drummed her fingers on the armrest of the couch, her eyes darting from one corner of the room to another.

She'd ended up here because she was needed, but that wasn't really the case anymore. She had midterms to study for, and her roommate was probably worried about her. It was time for her to go.

Bobbi got up and grabbed her coat. With a swift stride, she crossed the room and flung open the front door, desperate for fresh air.

The cool night breeze washed over her flushed skin, sending shivers down her spine. She took a deep breath, the crisp scent of autumn leaves calming her restless mind. She started walking towards her truck parked not far from the house, its body gleaming like a beacon of freedom under the moonlight.

"Hey, you're leaving?" Sarah called out from the doorway, curiosity lacing her voice.

"Can't stay cooped up here forever," Bobbi replied, trying to keep her voice steady. "Got things to do, you know?"

"Be careful, alright?" Sarah warned, her tone softening with concern.

"Always am," Bobbi said with a grin. "Have Mia or Riley give you my number. I like you Sarah. I hope I see you again."

As she approached her truck, the gravel crunched beneath her boots, each step feeling heavier than the last. She slid into the driver's seat, gripping the steering wheel tightly. She felt bad for not saying goodbye to Mia, but she didn't want to interrupt whatever weird conversation Mia was having with the vampire lady who owned the house.

"Come on, Bobbi," she whispered to herself, taking a deep breath. "You've got this."

Her hand shook as she pushed the start button for the ignition, the familiar hum of the engine offering little comfort. As she glanced in the rear window, her heart nearly stopped.

A group of figures emerged from the shadows, their eyes glowing like embers in the darkness. The hunger radiating from them was palpable, a sinister energy that sent shivers down her spine. Bobbi's heart pounded against her chest as she realized exactly what was happening. Glancing in the rear view mirror, the figures appeared to vanish.

Vampires. They were vampires.

"Shit," she hissed, her fingers tightening around the wheel. "I've got to warn them."

Bobbi's pulse raced as she flung open the door to her truck and hopped out, her feet hitting the ground hard. Her heart thudded against her ribcage as she grabbed her rifle from the gun rack mounted in the back.

"Move faster, Bobbi," she muttered under her breath, her voice barely audible above the cacophony of chirping crickets. Clenching the smooth wooden stock, she yanked out a box of ammo from beneath the seat and slammed the door shut.

Bobbi sprinted towards the house, gravel crunching beneath her boots, determination coursing through her veins like molten fire. Bursting through the front door, she found Sarah still sitting in the living room.

"Vampires!" Bobbi yelled, her voice cracking from urgency. "A lot of them. Outside. Right now."

"Shit," Sarah whispered, her fingers gripping the armrests of her chair. "Someone must have seen me leaving Carson's townhouse and followed me here. Lock the front door, I'll get the back door and grab Mia."

"And then?" Bobbi said, loading her rifle as quickly as possible.

"Then we get ready for a siege," Sarah replied, running out of the room.

Chapter 17

The temperature seemed to drop as Mia stood in the dimly lit foyer of Lucy's Victorian house. Her breath caught in her throat, her heart pounding with anticipation. A cacophony of snarls and hisses erupted outside.

"Showtime," she muttered quietly, her fingers twitching with pent-up energy.

"Stay focused, Mia," Sarah snapped, her eyes blazing.

"What the hell was unfocused about that." Mia rolled her eyes. She concentrated on the door, mumbling an incantation under her breath. A faint glow seeped from her sigil tattoos, intertwining with the ancient words she spoke. The door shimmered, its wood groaning as it absorbed the magical reinforcement.

"Nice trick," Emma said, seemingly bracing herself. "Let's see how long it holds."

"If we're lucky, until sunrise," Lucy replied, the creases of a frown crossing her otherwise lineless face. "Though we're rarely lucky."

Tell me about it, Mia thought, though she kept that sentiment to herself. She mentally prepared herself for battle, her pulse quickening. "I'm operating at about fifty percent power right now, so I have no idea how well this'll work."

"Bobbi, you in position?" Lucy called out, her voice echoing through the house.

"Almost there," Bobbi's voice crackled through a walkie-talkie.

Bobbi slid down the shingles of the old Victorian home's rooftop, barely stopping herself from falling off of the steep angled surface. Bracing herself against the side of the house's turret, she raised and aimed her rifle at the oncoming horde below. "I'm in position."

"Good. Keep an eye out and don't hesitate to shoot," Lucy instructed, her tone grave as it crackled on the radio on Bobbi's belt. "You won't kill them, but it will certainly slow them down."

"Piece of cake, like shooting a ten pointer on Sunday morning of deer camp," Bobbi quietly said to herself, pulling the trigger.

As if on cue, the reinforced door shuddered violently under the force of the attacking vampires, their bloodlust palpable even through the barrier. Mia stood her ground, her muscles tensing, and felt a surge of power course through her veins.

"They are... stronger than I expected..." Mia said through gritted teeth. "Not sure how much longer this'll hold."

"Then we'll be ready for what happens if it doesn't," Lucy replied, her eyes narrowing into slits. "With Carson gone, I might be able to exert my will over them. But I don't know if I can control a group this large."

"So we need to thin the herd," Mia said, nodding. "Got it. On the other hand –"

Mia was interrupted by the frame around the door exploding, sending shards of broken wood and glass into the room. Mia was knocked back as though she was punched in the stomach.

"About damn time," Emma hissed, lunging at the first vampire that crossed the threshold.

Mia regained her footing, and summoned an orb of fire in her hands, hurling it at an approaching attacker. He shrieked as flames consumed his body, leaving nothing but ash in his wake.

Several of the vampires dropped as they approached the house, knocked down by Bobbi's expert shooting.

"Nice shot," Jayla's voice chimed in from over the radio. "But maybe try aiming for the head or heart next time."

"Somebody's always a critic," Bobbi responded, her voice crackling over the walkie talkies.

Blood and sweat mingled in the air as the symphony of snarls, grunts, and gunfire filled every corner of the house. With each vampire that fell, another two seemed to take its place, amplifying the intensity of the battle.

"Jayla," Mia gasped between blows, "how many are left?"

"Sevente... no, wait −" Jayla's voice came through the intercom, her breaths labored from exertion. "Eighteen. They keep coming."

"Great," Mia muttered under her breath, just as a vampire lunged at her. She managed to dodge the attack, feeling the cold brush of death graze her cheek. Her heart raced with a mix of fear and exhilaration coursing through her veins. She couldn't help but wonder if this was what it felt like to be truly alive.

"Emma, watch your back!" Jayla warned through the intercom. Emma spun around, catching an attacking vampire by the throat and snapping its neck with a sickening crack.

"Riley, can you make sure the door to Jayla's room is secured?" Lucy shouted, her voice laced with frustration as she tore into another acolyte, sending him crashing into a group of approaching vampires.

"Bolted and locked," Riley replied. "And I'm currently putting as many heavy things as I can find behind it to blockade us up here. I won't let anyone hurt your girl."

"Thank you," Lucy said quietly. "I don't know what I would do if anything happened to her."

"Stay alive yourself," Riley radioed back. "What you two have may be fucked up and weird, but it's also cute and sweet and I'm kind of obsessed with it."

"Get off the channel, Riley!" Sarah snarled. "Jayla, any more on the second floor?"

"There's one... that I think is hiding in the bathroom?" Jayla's voice crackled. "I saw it go in, but the camera turns off in there when the door is closed."

"On it," Sarah responded, bolting down the hall.

"Lucy! How are you feeling!" Mia called out, dodging another vampire's futile attempt to sink its fangs into her flesh. "Have we gotten their numbers down enough?"

"Perhaps," Lucy mused, her voice calm amidst the chaos. "But I'll need cover."

"Leave that to us," Mia replied, determination igniting within her. "Ready?"

"Always," Lucy answered with a predatory grin.

"Alright, everyone, let's give Lucy some space!" Mia shouted, deftly maneuvering her self out of another vampire's reach.

Lucy's crimson eyes flashed with determination as she surveyed the chaos unfolding around her. The air was thick with the smell of sweat and the crackling energy of Mia's spells. Her heart, long dead but still capable of feeling, began to pound again in her chest with a mix of adrenaline and anticipation.

"Enough!" Lucy roared, channeling her vampiric power into the word. Her voice cut through the cacophony of snarls and screams like a razor-sharp blade, demanding the attention of everyone present. A wave of pressure pulsed through the undead horde, echoing down to the very bone.

At once, the battle seemed to freeze, as if time itself had bowed to Lucy's command. She could feel the weight of countless eyes upon her, each assessing her authority and calculating their next move. But Lucy didn't waver; she held her ground, her slender figure radiating an aura of strength and poise that belied her delicate appearance.

"Stand down," Lucy ordered, her voice firm yet laced with an undercurrent of menace. "I am your elder and you must obey."

The acolyte vampires hesitated, torn between their primal instincts and the allure of Lucy's otherworldly influence. For a moment, it seemed as though they might defy her, but then one by one, they lowered their heads in submission.

"Dammit, Lucy," Emma breathed, her voice tinged with awe. "You couldn't have done that twenty minutes ago?"

"Needed there to be a lot fewer of them," Lucy replied in hushed tones, and it was clear she was quietly shaking. "This is a lot harder than it looks, and if I fall I need you to catch me. I am very much at my limit right now."

Every eye in the house was on Lucy, and you could practically hear a pin drop.

"Listen to me," Lucy said, her voice soft but no less commanding. "I understand that you have been misled, manipulated by forces beyond your control. But I am here to help you, to guide you on a path away from darkness and destruction."

"Are we sure this is a good idea?" Sarah asked, her voice laced with skepticism. "We barely know these vampires, Lucy. We can't be certain they won't turn on us the first chance they get."

"Trust me," Lucy responded, her gaze never leaving the acolytes. "I can appeal to their better angels... and if that doesn't work I can go the pragmatic route."

Lucy looked around her, raising her voice. "I know you're scared, that you don't know what your way forward is. We've taken away the one guidepost you had. But if you continue down this road, you'll do nothing but guarantee that every vampire is hunted down and killed. The humans *will* come for you, and it never goes well for our kind when they do."

It was clear the young vampires were considering what she was saying. She just needed to to finish.

"I can help you, I can train you," Lucy said. "You might even lead lives where you can step into the daylight again. I just need you to let me."

The air in the room quivered with tension as Lucy's command hung ominously over the attacking vampires. Their eyes, once filled with bloodlust, now flickered with uncertainty and fear. It was a palpable shift, like the moment a storm recedes to reveal a fragile calm.

"Please," she whispered, allowing her voice to soften but still maintaining the force behind her words. "Let me help you."

As if on cue, one of the acolyte vampires stepped forward, his gaze locked on Lucy. The defiance that had previously marked his features now seemed to wane, replaced by a hesitant curiosity. He dropped to one knee, his head bowed in submission, and the others followed suit. A collective sigh seemed to pass through the room as the gravity of their surrender settled in.

"Thank you," Lucy said, her voice barely audible yet clear enough for everyone to hear. She approached the kneeling vampires and extended her hand towards the leader, her fingers brushing lightly against the side of his face.

"Your name?" Lucy asked, her presence commanding respect without the need for intimidation.

"Callum," he replied, raising his eyes to meet hers. He was just a kid, no older than twenty.

"Listen closely, Callum," Lucy instructed, her tone gentle yet firm. "You must learn to control your urges, to embrace the power within you without giving in to its darker temptations. I will guide you and your companions, but you must trust me. Can you do that?"

Callum hesitated for a heartbeat before nodding solemnly.

"Good," she said, smiling reassuringly. "Now rise. All of you rise."

As Callum and the others stood, Lucy turned to face her friends, their expressions a mixture of relief and concern. Mia only realized now she'd been holding her breath, and slowly let herself exhale.

"From this moment on, we are one," Lucy declared. "Together, we will navigate the treacherous path ahead and emerge stronger for it."

"Are you certain about this?" Emma questioned, her voice laced with doubt but also curiosity.

"Trust me," Lucy responded, her eyes filled with conviction. "I see in them the same spark that I saw in you, Emma. We must give them the chance to change, just as you were given."

"Alright," Emma conceded, her features softening. "I'll follow your lead. Not sharing a room though."

Lucy laughed to herself, nodded to her student.

"What's happening," Bobbi's voice crackled over the radio. "Is everyone okay?"

"They're fine," Jayla's voice crackled back. "Lucy ended the fight."

"That's... that's great?" Bobbi responded. "So, uh, can someone find a way to get me down from here then?"

Chapter 18

Mia's boots crunched on gravel as she entered the secluded park, the shadows of gnarled trees swallowing her whole. Moonlight filtered through the dense canopy above, casting eerie patterns upon the damp earth. She paused, breathing in the scent of wet moss and decaying leaves; it reminded her of things that were once alive but now lay dormant.

"Of all the places," a voice murmured from the darkness. "You chose the creepiest one."

"It's where I feel at home I guess," Mia said, her voice as soft as the night air. "Thank you for coming, Sarah."

Sarah Masters emerged from the shadows, looking like a specter bathed in moonlight. Her eyes locked onto Mia's, seeming to pierce straight through her carefully constructed façade. A shiver raced down Mia's spine – not from the chill in the air, but from the intensity of their shared gaze.

"Are you going to stand there, or are we going to talk?" Sarah asked, folding her arms across her chest.

Mia sighed, feeling the weight of their past pressing down upon her. "Yeah," she muttered, finding a nearby bench and sitting down. "Let's talk. I thought that maybe now that the world isn't burning down we should have the conversation we've been both avoiding since you showed up here. What happened in Boston and why I left."

"Feels like a lifetime ago," Sarah said softly, joining Mia on the bench. Her eyes seemed distant, lost in memories better left undisturbed.

"Maybe it was," Mia mused, staring up at the silvery slivers of moonlight. "But that doesn't mean we can forget what happened. The destruction we caused – both to ourselves and each other. What you gave up to save me."

"I don't regret that by the way," Sarah replied, her voice tinged with sadness. "I would have given up anything to save you, and I'd probably do it again. We save each other. It's what we do."

"I just wish that the thing I'd needed saving from wasn't caused by my own stupidity," Mia sighed, leaning back on the bench.

"Don't forget arrogance," Sarah said, shaking her head. "And it was both of us. We both decided to go through with it. We are all results of the choices we make."

"Oh I know that for sure," Mia said, a small smile crossing her lips. "And some of those choices leave you covered in sigil tattoos and a lingering sense of self-loathing."

"Ah, yes, the sigils…" Sarah smiled, glancing over at Mia's extensive tattoos. "Certainly a choice. Maybe a bit of an overreaction?"

"Maybe," Mia whispered, staring at the markings etched into her skin. "I guess when you feel that powerless, sometimes you do whatever you can to reclaim it."

"Sometimes I wonder if that night in the warehouse will ever truly leave us," Sarah admitted, her voice barely audible.

The words hung in the air, the silence only broken by the rustle of wind through the autumn leaves.

"God, Sarah," Mia whispered, her voice trembling with the force of emotions she could no longer contain. "That night… It was like I was drowning, like a torrent of darkness and malice was pulling me under."

The moonlight danced off her tear-streaked cheeks, creating a kaleidoscope of sorrow that mirrored the turmoil within. Mia drew in a shuddering breath, her gaze locked onto Sarah's.

"Sometimes when I close my eyes, I'm back there again. I can feel the cold wind cutting through me, the demonic laughter echoing in my ears. And the worst part is, I still crave it sometimes." Mia's admission hung heavily in the air, casting a somber pall over the scene.

"I know," Sarah said, placing her hand on Mia's arm. "I sometimes wake up in the middle of the night, drenched in sweat, my heart pounding because I'm terrified of the person I've become since then."

Mia searched for the right words, desperately wanting to provide some semblance of solace or understanding. But all she could do was nod mutely, knowing that no words would ever fully capture exactly what both of them were feeling.

"Sometimes, I wonder if I'll ever be whole again," Sarah confessed, her voice cracking with raw emotion. "If I'll ever be more than just a broken shell of the person I once was."

"Maybe we're both a little broken," Mia admitted, her own pain resonating with Sarah's. "But I think that's part of what makes us human."

"Is it?" Sarah asked, her voice barely audible. "Or is it just a cruel reminder of the monsters we let ourselves become?"

"Maybe it's both?" Mia suggested, her heart aching as she looked upon the woman she once loved so fiercely.

"But maybe, just maybe, we can use our broken pieces to build something better. Something stronger."

"Maybe," Sarah conceded, her eyes searching Mia's for a glimmer of hope. "But in order to do that, we have to confront what's inside us. And I'm not sure if either of us are ready for that."

"Guess we won't know until we try," Mia replied softly, her hand reaching out to brush against Sarah's, the warmth of their shared connection bittersweet in its intensity.

Mia stood and walked closer to the tree line. "I still don't know how to apologize for what I cost you. What you had to give up to save me."

"It was my choice," Sarah said, rising to her feet and following close behind. "And if it weren't for me, you would have never have started down that path to begin with."

"We walked it together," Mia sighed, leaning against a tree. "We both made that decision."

"True," Sarah admitted, her voice barely audible above the rustling leaves. "But I can't help wondering what our lives would be if we had chosen something else. Things weren't easy before that, but they were simpler."

"When we were two kids scraping by, barely surviving," Mia mused, her heart constricting at the thought of their love being tainted by the very demons they sought to escape. "We clung to each other because we didn't have anyone else."

"Imagine if those kids had just been allowed to be happy," Sarah said, shaking her head. "What if we'd lived in a world we didn't need to try and escape."

"I wish we'd been given that grace," Mia replied, feeling the heaviness in her chest grow. "I've thought about it a million times, but I need to apologize for how I left. You were hurt, and I walked out the door."

"You only walked out that door because I held it open for you," Sarah said, looking at the ground. "I shut you out entirely when you refused to give up magic. I pushed you away."

"Yeah, but I didn't have to disappear," Mia said, her voice barely a whisper. "I could have at least talked to you. I could have told you where I was going."

"I don't know that I would have listened," Sarah said. "You did what you needed to do to survive. I don't think I understood that for a long time, and I had a lot of anger about it."

Mia's fingers trailed along the rough bark of the tree, her mind racing as she tried to untangle the complexities of their relationship. "I deserved that anger," she admitted, her voice barely a whisper. "But I know I loved you. I don't think I've been willing to open up to anyone since."

"I loved you too," Sarah conceded, her eyes searching Mia's.

"God it's so good to see you," Mia choked out, her voice cracking as the weight of their emotions threatened to suffocate her. "I really didn't think I'd ever see you again."

"Neither did I," Sarah whispered, her thumb gently tracing circles on the back of Mia's hand. "I'm glad chance brought me here... and that we were able to talk."

"Was it chance, or was it something else," Mia said quietly.

The words hung heavy in the air, an unspoken acknowledgment that their individual paths to recovery would lead them away from one another. Mia felt a pang in her chest, a sharp ache that resonated with the knowledge that they might finally be about to part ways for good.

"Sarah," Mia began, her voice wavering, "I want you to know that I'll always cherish the time we spent together, the life we shared. The *love* we shared. But I also realize that we need to face our – and I swear to god I'm not making a pun – *demons* separately, to find our own sense of peace."

"I know," Sarah said softly, her eyes glistening with tears. "I've been thinking the same thing. We've both hurt each other in so many ways, and I don't want to risk causing you any more pain."

A sob caught in Mia's throat as she leaned forward, resting her forehead against Sarah's. She closed her eyes, allowing herself to fully absorb the raw vulnerability of this moment. Her thoughts raced, a cacophony of regrets, fears, and hopes for the future.

"Promise me something," Mia murmured, her breath hitching, "Promise me that no matter where this life takes you, you won't forget what we had."

"Never," Sarah said firmly, her voice thick with emotion. "I'll carry it with me, always. And I hope you will too."

Mia nodded, her tears spilling down her cheeks, mingling with Sarah's as they embraced one last time.

"Goodbye, Sarah," Mia whispered into her ear.

"Goodbye, Mia."

As they pulled apart, the moonlight seemed to intensify, bathing them in a luminous glow that marked both an ending and a beginning. But beneath the sorrow, there was also a sense of hope – a quiet belief that they would find healing, growth, and perhaps even redemption.

Chapter 19

The autumn sun cast a warm golden glow over Parrish Mills as the town returned to relative normalcy. Mia strolled along the downtown's sidewalks, inhaling the crisp autumn air as she passed families oblivious to the danger they had narrowly avoided. The sound of children's laughter filled the air, mingling with the scent of fresh-baked bread wafting from the corner bakery.

"Oh god, I've actually acclimated to this place. I like *live* here now," Mia muttered to herself, kicking a loose stone as she walked. She couldn't shake the feeling that her past would rear its head again, but for now she was happy to live in her cozy little town. If darkness was everywhere, you may as well like the way things looked when the sun was up.

"Mia! Slow your ass down!" A familiar voice called out, breaking her reverie. "Some of us aren't wearing the shoes for this kind of pace."

"Drink less booze, eat more vegetables," Mia replied with a sarcastic grin. "You can keep up, Riley."

"I haven't even had coffee yet, give a girl a break." Riley said, slightly out of breath.

"You know what's funny?" Mia scoffed. "We spent the last week almost getting killed to save all of these people, and they'll never know it happened."

"True, but would you want them to?" Riley reminded her gently. "I think I miss the days before I found out about all this spooky shit."

Mia sighed, her shoulders slumping slightly as she considered Riley's words. She ran her fingertips over one of her tattoos, feeling the thrum of power beneath her skin. "Yeah, I guess you're right. I can't imagine my life not knowing though."

"Well, you make it work for you," Riley said, placing a comforting hand on Mia's shoulder. "Honest to god, I'm jealous of how you take all this bullshit in stride."

"Thanks, Riley." Mia smirked. "We can't all be twenty-eight year old recovering addict high school drop outs who work retail."

"I know, it sucks. Some of us are just stuck with massive student debt taking jobs as college professors. I guess I'll just have to make do," Riley quipped. "Now, come on. Let's go grab some breakfast and pretend like we don't have a care in the world."

"Sounds good to me," Mia agreed, following her friend down the street..

"Listen, Mia, I know you're still kind of reeling after seeing Sarah" Riley said, her eyes filled with sincerity. "But I want you to know that I'm here for you, no matter what."

Mia felt the familiar warmth of gratitude surge through her chest, knowing that she could always count on Riley. "Thanks, Riles. I truly don't know what I'd do without you."

"Probably get into even more trouble than you already do," Riley teased, nudging Mia playfully with her elbow. "Now come on, I need caffeine, stat."

Riley led Mia towards their usual coffee shop, its bright interior adorned with local band posters and walls mysteriously stained nicotine yellow, even though smoking in cafés had been banned for over a decade. The bell above the door jingled merrily as they stepped inside, greeted by the sweet aroma of fresh grounds.

Mia winked at the cute dark haired barista in a short skirt, leading Riley to roll her eyes.

"You just can't turn it off, can you," Riley laughed.

Mia shrugged, "Hey, I've got to use all my assets." She leaned over the counter and whispered something in the barista's ear. The other woman blushed and giggled in response.

Riley rolled her eyes again, "Leave the new girl alone, Mia. God, why do I put up with you?"

Mia laughed, "Because you love me." She turned back to the barista, "Can we get two large coffees and a couple of those pumpkin muffins?"

"Sure thing," the barista said with a smile, jotting down their order.

As the barista went to make drinks, Mia turned to Riley, "You know she's not new, right? Stacy's friends with Bobbi, and she's been serving us coffee like three times a week for the last six months."

"I... six months? I haven't noticed that girl for six months?" Riley said in disbelief. "What happened to Carla?"

"Carla quit and moved to Chicago last June?" Mia laughed, shaking her head. "You need to get your head in the game, Dr. Whittaker."

"Apparently," Riley said, shaking her head.

After a few minutes, they sat down with their coffees at a nearby table.

"I'm really glad you came to this town, you know," Riley said softly, her voice tinged with affection. "I think we make quite the team."

"Me too," Mia agreed, her heart swelling with love for her best friend. "And who knows? Maybe we actually make a difference."

"Oh, we all know what your 'making a difference' entails," Riley quipped, grinning mischievously as they sipped their coffees.

After an hour, Mia and Riley got up and wandered over to the bustling Farmer's Market. The aroma of fresh produce and baked goods filling the air of that season's final market. Mia couldn't help but marvel at how blissfully untroubled the residents of Parrish Mills seemed. She envied them.

"You ever wonder how many people around you aren't just people?" Riley pondered. "I went on a date with a vampire. How many other things that go bump in the night have I run across and just not known it?"

"Vampires, werewolves, and other assorted supernatural madness..." Mia pondered. "There's a lot out there."

"Yeah... wait," Riley said, pausing. "Did you say 'werewolf?' Are werewolves real too?"

"I don't know what you're talking about," Mia said, attempting to put on an innocent face. She slowly backed away into the market crowd.

"You have to tell me if werewolves are real, Mia Graves!" Riley said, stalking after her friend. "You tell me right this instant!"

****

Lucy's large once quiet Victorian house now bustled with energy, as Emma assisted her in navigating the chaos brought on by their new charges.

"Focus!" Lucy barked, her eyes locked onto a young man struggling to control his newfound strength. "You need to learn restraint!"

"Easy for you to say, you've been doing this for centuries," he grumbled, rubbing his arm where he'd accidentally punched a hole in the wall.

"Centuries of practice," Lucy reminded him sharply. "Now, try again."

As the fledgling vampires attempted to master their abilities, Emma prowled among them like a hawk, her eyes constantly scanning for signs of trouble. Though she was still a newcomer herself, she had embraced her role as Lucy's right hand with an almost frightening zeal.

"Doing great, guys," Emma encouraged, clapping one of the new vampires on the back. "Just remember that humans are friends, not food."

"Did you just quote A Shark's Tale?" the young vampire asked incredulously.

"No, I quoted Finding Nemo. Keep up Dave," Emma replied, rolling her eyes.

Lucy ducked away from the crowd, unlocking the hidden door and trudging up the narrow staircase to the attic. The cacophony of voices from below almost drove her mad, and she needed a break. The weight of her responsibilities threatened to crush her down into dust, and she longed for a quiet moment away from the chaos. As she reached the top, the wooden door creaked open, revealing Jayla's mischievous grin.

"Escaping the madness?" Jayla asked, stretching languidly across the plush sofa that occupied the Northern wall of the attic.

"Only temporarily," Lucy sighed, sinking onto the floor beside her. "I just need a moment of peace."

"Or you could just stay up here with me all the time," Jayla joked, running her fingers through Lucy's hair with a teasing smile. "I promise I can find ways to help you relax."

"Believe me, the thought has crossed my mind," Lucy admitted, closing her eyes as Jayla's touch sent shivers down her spine.

"You haven't eaten today, have you," Jayla said with concern. She climbed down onto the floor next to Lucy, meeting her eyes. "And you look exhausted."

"Can I take a nap up here with you?" Lucy said, pleadingly.

"You're... asking?" Jayla said. "Oh hon, you really are exhausted. Take those shoes off, get in the bed, and I'll pretend you're the big bad predator so you can get some sleep."

"I don't know how I'd survive this without you, Jayla," Lucy sighed, getting to her feet and stumbling towards the bed.

"You probably wouldn't," Jayla laughed, pulling off Lucy's shoes as the vampire sat on the edge of mattress. "Now you just relax, and I'll whisper lovely things in your ear about how scary you are."

"That'd be nice, Jayla... that'd be nice."

****

Mia pushed open the door to Markov Books. A bell chimed overhead, announcing her arrival. The dimly lit interior was a comforting embrace, the musty aroma of old books intermingling with the faint trace of incense. An assortment of crystals glinted in the low light, while shelves

192

groaned under the weight of mass produced witchcraft books.

"Ah, Mia," a velvety voice called from behind a towering stack of books. "You're just in time. I have something for you."

Mia glanced up, her eyes locking with those of Zelda Markov, the enigmatic owner of the bookstore. She was an elegant woman with her long silver hair pulled into a tight bun. Her piercing gaze seemed to see straight through Mia, leaving her feeling both unnerved and intrigued.

"Zelda, what's up? You actually came in for once." Mia commented, trying to maintain her composure despite the unsettling sensation crawling beneath her skin.

"Here, my dear." Zelda produced a small, leather-bound book, its cover etched with arcane symbols. "I ran across this and I thought it might be up your alley."

Mia hesitated, her fingers trailing over the intricate designs. She could feel a subtle energy pulsing from the worn pages, and as she opened the book, the words seemed to dance before her eyes.

"Thank you," she whispered, her voice barely audible even in the hushed atmosphere of the store. "Is this... is this the Grimoire of Arcanus? I've been searching for a copy of this for a while."

"Your journey has been a difficult one, Mia, and I don't just mean how bad you are at locating rare books for yourself," Zelda said gently, her eyes filled with empathy. "But this place, this town... it has given you the strength to face your demons, both literal and metaphorical. You have found a sense of purpose here, and I am glad we have played a small part in that."

"What are you talking about, Zelda?" Mia asked.

"You dealt with the whole vampire thing," Zelda said, gesturing loosely with her left hand. "Which was nice, because it meant *I* didn't have to deal with the whole vampire thing."

Mia stopped in her tracks. "You knew about that?"

"There were a bunch of vampires running around, way more than normal," Zelda said with a shrug. "Kind of hard not to notice. Frankly, you being around has been really convenient. It's been nice not having to get my hands dirty. So thanks."

"Uh, you're welcome?" Mia said cautiously. "I like being here?"

Zelda offered a knowing smile, her eyes shining with warmth. "I like having you here too. Also, Mike quit last night, so I'm making you the new manager. I need you to hire some additional staff ASAP."

"I'm what?" Mia said incredulously.

"Oh don't act surprised," Zelda smiled. "You were doing like half the job already. I need to run, but I'll be back this evening to cover Mike's shift. Please hire someone fast so I don't have to keep coming in to work?"

Mia nodded as Zelda slipped out the door, leaving her alone in the store. She smiled to herself, and walked to the back. She stood in the doorway of what was, apparently, her new office for a moment before walking to the boxes that were the previous night's delivery. Sitting on top of the stack of packages was a small special order. Mia picked it up, and looked at it in her hands. It was Nic's tarot deck. It had finally arrived.

Mia stood for a moment, just staring at the box of cards.

"I'll do a reading for you, Nic," Mia said quietly to the empty room.

About the Author

Trae Dorn is just your average geeky, nonbinary genderqueer witch. They live just on the edge of the woods somewhere in Wisconsin with their spouse.

They are the creator of the comics UnCONventional and Peregrine Lake. They also run the Nerd & Tie Podcast Network where they host a number of shows including the popular witchcraft podcast BS-Free Witchcraft.

They are also very, very tired.

You can find more about them at **traedorn.com**